DEVOURING THE DEMON

THE FAEVERSE CHRONICLES

HUNTER J. SKYE

1

HUMAN

I peered into the bathroom mirror and stretched the rainbows over my skin until they shrink-wrapped my glamour in place. Maryland was a "glamour-intact state" so my human form had to be on display at all times. *I know the differentiation isn't all that important to you humans, but it can be a matter of life and death to the fae.* We all had to memorize which states were glamour-intact, which were glamourless, and which were glamour-apparent. If we even drive through a glamourless state—like say Utah—with our appearance altering magic on, it's perfectly legal for humans to shoot at us. *Actually, if we show our true forms there, someone might pop off a few rounds as well, so maybe Utah isn't a good example.*

How about my home state, Maryland? This is a glamour-intact state. If I were to walk down the street, here in Baltimore, in all my bare Lilith glory—pale blue skin, metallic silver eyes, light-drinking sable hair, six-inch owl talons carving up the asphalt, I'd be arrested. Worse, the human authorities would turn me over to the Council, our governing body of blood-thirsty Old-World fae. The Council didn't bother with things like judges and juries. There was no defending myself in a comfy court of law. If I found myself in front of the Council for any infraction, my fate was already sealed. I'd be sent to the Wells for some quality time with the Soul Seepers—parasitic creatures capable of, among other gruesome things, making a fae's skin weep mana. Irreplaceable energy that, once taken, was gone for good. At least, that's how it usually went, but strangely, a month ago, I'd been dragged to the bottom of the Underhill—our sentient, underground biome in Baltimore—and subjected to an unusual Council inquiry. The whole horrifying encounter had resulted in my immediate, forced two-week vacation, which was still happening six weeks later. No Soul Seepers. No punishment at all. Just sunny beaches, mai tais, and a muddy, snake-infested tryst which had left me with more life force than my body could hold.

"You okay in there?" Daniel's muffled voice softened with compassion. *Yes, that Daniel. The handsome human I can't have, but can't seem to stay away from. The Daniel I almost killed in the staff lounge when I gave into my desires for a mere moment.*

"I'm fine." I didn't sound fine. My voice cracked like old plaster.

I tugged at the fraying lavender edges around my face. I'd been gone from the Underhill too long. My glamour was thinning. Bits of blue skin shadowed the edges of my hairline. Onyx black streaks marred my glossy brown waves. My faeness was beginning to show. All I'd ever dreamed of was to get out of that grumpy pile of rocks we fae called home. There were other underhills in the world that were far less ornery, but I'd landed in the Maryland one, which was arguably the worst behaved pocket universe of the fae realm.

And now that I wanted back in, it was closed.

Shut down for the season.

Sealed shut with an arc welder.

I couldn't even break in with a jackhammer. *Yes, I've tried.* Something had happened in the earth under Hans Jodkins University's lab for Functional Anatomy and Evolution. The interdimensional apertures that linked our bad-tempered locus geographia to the human laboratories above ground had disappeared. Either Domov and his portal-opening brethren had gone on strike or the Council had closed the connection. The last message I'd received was to "stay away." That was it. I couldn't reach Daphne, my supervisor and best friend. I couldn't reach my co-workers. No phone calls, texts, nothing.

I was stranded.

"Do you want a glass of water?" Daniel drummed his fingers on the door frame of his bathroom nervously.

"No, thanks," I whispered through parched lips.

I washed my hands with the new orange-blossom soap we'd purchased at the Farmer's Market then splashed some water on my mostly human face. I dabbed it with a towel. The bright, citrus fragrance revived me a little.

The egg timer I'd set for three minutes chimed from its spot on the back of Daniel's toilet.

The moment had come.

This was it.

Do or die.

Literally.

Just look.

Lilith, look.

I stared at my reflection. Anxiety stirred the rainbows clinging to my skin. They flashed and sparked along my full lips. They shimmered down the long sweep of my nose. I looked scared. Correction—I looked terrified.

I took a deep breath and glanced down at the closed lid of the toilet.

My heart stuttered.

I stared at the human pregnancy test in utter disbelief. The fae didn't have pregnancy tests, so I'd waited an entire month for my potential pregnancy hormones to match the levels of a human woman. And now the wait was over. Two faint pink lines.

"Lilith?"

Daniel knew about my potential baby predicament, but he didn't know what that meant for me as a Lilith. My birthing curse wasn't exactly a topic for the dinner table. How does a girl work into conversation that she can't keep a child until she's killed one hundred of her previous offspring? It was a savagery only the Father Who Turned Away could remove from my kind.

I tried to calm my breathing, but my head spun like a carousel. Those two faint lines on the tester stick represented all my hopes and all my fears. They were my past, my ancestry, and my future. My very short future. Those lines were life and death. If I didn't kill the child after its first breath, I would die. The curse would hunt me down and end me. Just like my mother.

"Lilith, open the door."

Of all the different genetic phyla and classes and families of fae humans had learned of twenty years ago during the Revelation, Liliths were a genus humans just couldn't get enough of. We fae didn't have rock stars, or social media celebrities. We had demons and dragons, hags and trolls, and—yes—we had sex fairies. I was a walking, talking wet dream which absolutely no human could have sex with.

As a Lilith or, as the Talmud had labeled us, a Night Monster, my special genitals were designed to drain my lover's life force.

No, I still won't show you. Quit asking.

As it was, only the strongest of fae could mate with me, and that was iffy now that I'd consumed an unfathomable amount of mana. *Note to self: don't fuck an immortal in the Everglades. Don't fuck an immortal anywhere, ever again.* There was definitely no way Daniel and I could do the deed, no matter how badly we wanted to.

We'd spent four long weeks eating takeout, playing darts, and discussing everything but our feelings for each other. I knew so much about his family now that it felt like I'd been there in the treehouse with him and his sisters as they'd planned to build a rocket ship. I could almost see the brightly-colored Easter eggs that had fallen down gopher holes in the backyard or feel the chest-shaking explosions of the Fourth of July fireworks over the lake behind his childhood home.

He knew things about me too. I'd told him about my first trip through the Ways, the inner roads that led to other underhills. How small and frightened I'd been. Each universe of faerie had its own wonders and dangers. He'd listened to them all. He'd hung on every word of my stories about navigating the human world as well. He'd made me feel brave, like an adventurer. Not like a motherless drifter lost among her own kind. He'd played the part of supportive friend, but our hugs were too long, our laughter too nervous, our glances too furtive.

Yes, I was attracted to that tall, tanned bone-digger, but I liked his brain too. It helped that we were both anthropologists. Well, he was an anthropologist. I worked for the fae genetics lab connected to Hans Jodkins University's Laboratory for Functional Anatomy and Evolution. Our interspecies partnership was set up to share information. We helped humans with their research, at least on the surface of things. But they didn't know about our breeding project. The Council of Elders was hard at work reconstituting the fae population by recombining genes through forced copulation.

So, if you have even a drop of fae blood, you best keep it to yourself or you'll be paired with a full-blooded fae of your species and forced to fuck. Yep, old school. While we watch.

Though neither of us had voiced it, we'd both been hoping my test would be negative. We'd already fooled ourselves into thinking there was a way a human and a Lilith could be intimate without the ensuing loss of life. Now that I'd received a giant upgrade in mana reserves, my eros was almost surely lethal to a human. And, on top of that...I was pregnant.

"I'm coming out." I flushed the toilet and took my time washing my trembling hands.

We'd discussed the differences in our life cycles several times. We'd quietly faced the fact that I was much longer lived than he. Eventually, he'd grow old and die and if we were still together, I'd potentially mourn him for centuries.

Boy, had the tables turned. Two little lines had just reversed our fates. Unless he got hit by a bus or something, Daniel would out-live me by fifty years at least.

"I know this is difficult," Daniel's gentle voice strained, "but I think you have a message."

"A message?" I yanked the bathroom door open. The sudden whoosh of air blew his sun-bleached, cookie brown hair into his eyes.

He tucked the chin length strands behind his ear and nodded nervously.

"Where is it?" I looked at his empty hands.

"On the floor."

I searched the hardwood of the bedroom floor for a piece of paper. I checked the rug for an envelope. I found nothing.

Then, Daniel pointed to the fireplace, where the remains of last night's fire still glowed. A wisp of smoke danced along the wood in front of the fireplace tiles, and that's when I saw it. Several embers had jumped out of the grate and burned a little, glowing message into his black walnut flooring.

Lilith,

Bring the Swamp Witch.

Hurry!

-Hamus

Hamus! That judgmental, tyrannical, poorly-dressed prick! I had half a mind to pull up the floorboards, flip them over, and ignore the draco-demon's message. If it had to do with Hamus, I wasn't interested. In fact, nothing about Hamus interested me...except maybe the way his fire-licked hair seemed to flicker brighter when I entered a room. Or the way his ruddy firelight danced off his opalescent scales like the aurora borealis. Or the way his chainmail skirt rode up sometimes, providing a quick glimpse of his best asset.

Hamus had a legendary cock which he had used to sire many lines of fae. But those days were gone. He hadn't taken a lover since his wife had died nearly a century ago. He was strictly *look but don't touch* now. Especially for me. Hamus hated Liliths and me in particular, though I had no idea why.

"Swamp Witch?" Daniel eyed the sooty message.

"I don't know a swamp witch."

"It sounds urgent." He casually stomped on the sizzling message as if it were a normal thing for a human to encounter. *He's so cute when he tries.*

It did sound urgent, and since Hamus was a Council Member, I couldn't ignore his command.

My stomach turned.

I ran back to the bathroom.

Was it the pregnancy making me nauseous, or the thought of standing before that homicidal council of ancient monsters? Or was it the idea of seeing Hamus again after our strange far-seeing encounter last month when I'd been trapped and on the verge of death. And he'd been...nice.

Who was the Swamp Witch? How could I find her? And, why had Hamus reached out to me? He loathed me. He'd sooner kill me than work with me.

I'd missed something.

Something big.

2

AMERICAN ROCK DOVE

89% Domestic Dove

11% Mourning Dove

I closed the door gently on Daniel's concern, his comfort, his uncertainty, and his tender affection and perched on the lip of the bathtub. I needed a moment. I needed to sit alone with this new reality. I'd spent years complaining about the isolation of the Underhill, but now, when the threads of my life were unwinding, the only place I wanted to be was in my tiny room surrounded by walls of living rock looking up at the ribcage of a being that cared enough about us to give its body over as a dwelling place. Now, I was an underhill. I was the shelter. I was a dead woman.

Where had my fear flown to? Why had my sorrow slinked off? My panic was MIA as well. Those bright impulses belonged to a girl who no longer lived inside my skin. She'd packed her selfish obsessions and trivial bothers into her petty little suitcase and left without closing the door. Without looking back.

Now there was only me. Stripped down to bare walls and empty rooms, a shadowed hallway with a light at the end of it. In a matter of minutes, I'd transformed. And—*Lesser Gods, protect me*—I was happy.

Tears burned my eyes as those two faint pink lines whispered to me that I was not worthless. I was not a mistake of creation. The Father Who Turned Away might have deemed me unworthy of raising a child, but he had not forbidden me the joy of growing one.

Slowly, I stood and walked to the mirror. My mother's face greeted me in the glass. She looked with my eyes at the child she'd made. Though I'd never met her, she was with me somewhere behind our identical features. Somewhere in my heart.

My fingers drifted to my abdomen where a tiny soul slept, an entity barely perceptible, but there nonetheless.

"I'll be here for you as long as I can." I smiled and my tears blurred the bathroom. I was finally something more.

"Lilith, can we talk?"

"Yes." I laughed though nothing was funny. Was this contentment?

I opened the door and was treated to the Caribbean blue seas of Daniel's eyes. Not kidding, those eyes should have had pirate ships floating in them. Even heavy with worry his gaze still thrilled through me. Still spread a smile across my lips.

He hadn't—*how do you humans say*—run for the hills.

"I mean, we don't have to talk about that." He put his palms toward my belly as if my unborn child had a force-field around it. "But we probably should talk about that." He pointed at the singed floor.

"Yeah." I crossed to the bed and sat on the end.

"Maybe I can help." Daniel twisted the small fossil pendant hanging from a thong around his neck. He'd found it on his last dig and now it was his favorite fidget.

"You've already done so much, Daniel."

"It's my pleasure, but I know I can do more." He looked down and ran a square hand through his shaggy waves.

"Okay, then, if it's not too much to ask, could I get a ride to the mountains?"

"The mountains?"

"The Appalachian Mountain Range in West Virginia to be exact. There's someone living there I'd like to speak to."

"Am I allowed to know who?" He dropped the necklace. It thudded against his sternum.

"She's a Lilith like me, but much older. She's managed to stay off the Council's radar by living off grid in a remote piece of wilderness. I haven't spoken to her since I was a girl, but I could really use her advice now." My hand drifted over my waist. His eyes followed. "She's more likely to know the outlanders and nomads living outside of the underhills. If this Swamp Witch is fae, she will know of her."

"What if the witch is not fae?"

"Lilith will point us in the right direction. If not, then we will start with the closest swamps and work our way out until we find her."

"Okay." He nodded once and leaned against the wall. "I'll check online for references to a Swamp Witch. Maybe she has a website." He winked and that slow, rum bottle grin spread across his handsome face.

"Maybe she does." I grinned back. He pushed away from the wall and reached his hands toward me. I took them and let him pull me to my feet.

"Your hands are cold."

"My glamour is wearing thin." I looked down so that my hair would fall over the bluing edges of my face. "I've been away from the Underhill too long."

He let go of my left hand and placed his fingers under my chin to gently coax my face up. He looked at me. I looked at him. His gaze found the lavender blush at my hairline.

"You're beautiful." He said it like he meant it. "And lucky for you, I like my women chilly. You can hold my beer and keep it cold for me."

I rolled my eyes in mock annoyance, but I loved his ridiculous sense of humor. I also loved it when he spoke like I was his woman. And, I loved to say the word "love" in a sentence when thinking about him. There was a small part of me that would always hope for a future with Daniel.

My throat tightened and I wrapped my arms around him. I pressed my ear to his chest and listened to the comforting thump of his heart. His arteries whooshed with energy. His skin crackled with life. Daniel was a specimen of human male vitality. He was everything I was programmed to crave. And, as a Lilith, my succubus nature called to him in a voice his limbic system could not ignore.

Daniel's heart rate climbed. His skin flushed with heat.

My arms tightened.

His breathing increased. He buried his nose in my hair and inhaled.

A few weeks ago, that would have been the tipping point. I'd have flung him onto the bed, ripped the clothes from his hard, angular body, and skipped the foreplay. I'd already seen Daniel's cock. So, I knew just how I wanted to ride it. With my back tipped so I could enjoy every veiny inch.

Daniel's hand fastened on my jaw forcing my face up again, but this time the gaze I met wasn't playful. The jokes were gone. His eyes had lost their focus. His loose lips lowered toward mine. Desire washed over me. More than I'd ever sensed from him before.

My eros stirred.

"Daniel."

His hands fastened on my arms.

"Daniel. Easy."

He leaned into me. His feet found their way between mine and he used his knee to force my thighs apart.

"Daniel, it's after sunset. You know my eros is harder to control at night."

"I don't care." His voice churned like a gravel road. His breath warmed my ear. My neck.

My fingers curved into talons. The sharp hooks caught on his tee-shirt. His hands searched me like he had a map to the most tender spots.

"I—I can't. I'll hurt you." My voice came out breathy and lacking determination. I couldn't call on Domov to open a portal. I couldn't whisk away to my pocket universe and release my eros in the safety of my own domain. I had to manage moments like this or pick another couch to surf on.

His lips brushed my neck. I gripped him by the flimsy material of his shirt. Ready to fling him into the wall. Through the wall if I had to.

His thick, wet tongue spread across my pulse point. His calloused fingers rolled the tips of my breasts into hardened gems.

"No." I gasped.

Eros poured from me like a neglected fountain in a forgotten garden. It filled the room. The apartment. The entire brownstone. Shuddering shrieks sounded through the walls as Daniel's neighbors got their first taste of fae sex magic.

Daniel's body jerked and spasmed, but his hands still roamed. Still discovered. His fingers found their way past my shorts. They teased along the moistening edge of my undies. I gripped his wrist as he hovered dangerously close to the slippery wet seat of my power.

"Please," he begged. I'd ruined him again. I'd drowned his human brain in a tidal wave of lust until the happy, flirty, confident man I'd fallen for melted into a man-shaped shell of clamoring, covetous desire. Frankly, given my new power upgrade, I was surprised he was still standing.

I had to make a decision. Give in to what we both want, follow my instincts and fuck the life out of him. Or leave.

A quiet presence stirred on the eddies of my mana. My eros had woken the sleeper hiding in my womb. I was a creature of instinct. A monster. A slayer of men. But I was more. Now, I was more.

I twisted his tee-shirt until it was knotted in my talons, then I shook Daniel. Hard.

"We can't!" I caught his startled gaze. "We can never!" I pushed him toward the wall and leapt for the bedroom window. I yanked it open and dove into the violet night. My owl wings burst from my back ripping my tank top. I startled a pair of pigeons roosting on the ledge next to Daniel's window. They wouldn't be the only ones shocked to see a giant owl woman coasting through the city.

I caught the evening breeze in my feathers as the sidewalk rushed to meet me. A few strong beats and I was climbing into the night away from the fuck palace I'd just turned Daniel's apartment building into. Away from the human who reminded me constantly of the things I could not have.

My glamour hung in tatters. I was in direct violation of Baltimore's glamour-intact mandate. Anyone who stopped to look at the giant owl silhouette gliding on the last glowing rays of dusk could record a video or call the police. The ever-present anti-fae protestors camped out at the East Gate of the University would have a field day with this. I could be arrested, but that would be the least of my problems. If word of this incident reached the Council, I was done for. I'd gotten lucky the last time I'd been brought before them. There'd be no second chances.

I caught an updraft and let it take me high over the downtown area, high enough to see the river and the distant silhouette of the Francis Scott Key Bridge. High enough to see the dark green square of Patterson Park and the hulking complex of Hans Jodkins University and Hospital. Somewhere below it all, deep in the cold, quiet ground, the Underhill kept its secrets.

Unless the Council of Elders had fled the pocket universe before it closed and were now trapped in the human world with me, I don't think I had to worry about one small slip up. They had bigger problems than a glamourless Lilith loose in the night.

At least they were in the Faerie Lands—a series of connecting underhills—the place I always wanted to leave and now couldn't wait to get back to.

I turned and circled back in the direction of Daniel's building as the last of the light slipped from the horizon.

I guess we always want what we can't have.

3

SOUTHERN RUTABAGA PIXIE

67% Cruciferous

33% Insecta

It was all I'd ever dreamed of—driving down the road in Daniel's Jeep, top off—the Jeep, not my shirt—okay, mine too. Running my fingers through his wind-tossed hair, listening to his favorite human music. He'd flash me a smile and I'd melt into the moment, the belonging.

But this wasn't that moment. Yes, we were on the road. Daniel had taken the top off of his Jeep, and the wind was blowing his hair, but he hadn't looked at me once since we'd left Baltimore. My top was staying on and my fingers were definitely not in his hair. Add to it the fact that cars made me nauseous. Sitting this close to a combustible engine gave me the mother of all headaches. At least we weren't on the interstate anymore.

We'd made it to the West Virginia line without speaking about what had happened last night. Actually, we'd made it to a strange peninsula where the lines of West Virginia, Maryland, and Virginia all met. The triangular town of Harper's Ferry felt uncomfortably like a trine. It sat at the convergence of two great rivers. Both waterways were ancient and clumsy and studded with boulders. They created two watery walls of a triangle. Something unseen made the third. A road maybe. Or a ridge. I couldn't tell, but I could sense and what I was sensing was trapped energy.

"Can you drive around this town?" I broke the silence. I had to. I'd rather face Daniel's wrath over my behavior last night, than risk getting trapped in that shadowy little community.

He grunted and picked the left fork in the road which took us safely around the town. Signs for Civil War points of interest beckoned us to alter our route, but we weren't tourists on a holiday weekend. We weren't carefree lovers wandering through the countryside on a sunny day. And, as much as I wanted it, we never would be. But, even angry and hiding behind his mirrored sunglasses, Daniel was still my heart's desire. My infuriating, unattainable heart's desire.

"So, we're speaking now?" he grumbled.

"Sounds like it."

He shook his head as though he were absorbing my sass and compressing it into something heavier than it was.

"Does this mean you are finally going to explain why you jumped out of my bedroom window last night?"

"You know why I jumped out of the window."

"You put yourself in danger."

"I was endangering you."

"I was fine—" his voice reached a pitch I'd never heard from him before. His foot pressed a little harder on the gas and his fingers went to his fossil necklace. "Didn't you notice that I was fine?"

"You were not fine."

"My heart rate, my breathing, my mental state—all fine."

"I didn't see it that way."

"You were seeing what you wanted to see, not what was actually happening."

"Daniel—" my own voice leaped up an octave. "It's just—how do you humans say—wishy thinking."

"Wishful thinking. Wish full."

"Whatever. It's too dangerous for us to be together...like that."

"I'm not so sure. I'm not sure that you aren't using that as an excuse."

"An excuse?" I turned my whole body to face him because my entire being was curious to know what he meant by that. "An excuse for what?"

"You know."

"Enlighten me."

"A reason for us to not give this a real shot."

I blinked. My mouth hung open wide enough for a bug to fly in. I crunched on it and swallowed quickly before Daniel could notice.

Yuck, rutabaga pixie. The small, cruciferous insect was commonly mistaken for a crane fly—the bug you humans referred to as a mosquito hawk or "skeeter-eater". Not much meat, mostly wings.

So many emotions crowded in that I had to make them form a line. Anger over the accusation. Shock at how he could still be so clueless. And...wonder. Absolute wonder over the fact that he still wanted me. A pregnant monster who jumps out of windows. I blinked again. I braced as the last emotion in line stepped forward—sadness—as drowning as the swiftly flowing river next to us. Did he think I didn't want it too? A real shot.

"I'm trying to be realistic." The words came out in the form of a sob. My eyes welled with tears so quickly you would've thought I'd just been punched in the nose. *Oh, my Lesser Gods.* What was wrong with me? Another racking sob ripped from my quivering lips. This was what you humans called blubbering. I was blubbering.

Daniel's mouth hung low enough to collect a few bugs too. I didn't see him chewing so he must not have caught anything. He looked from me to the road to me again, then pulled over. He found a road cut with a cliff of exposed rock and a clearing wide enough to park the Jeep. We jerked to a stop. He put the Jeep in park and turned the engine off. The pain in my head shrank to a mild throbbing. A curtain of honeysuckle spilled over the sun-dappled road cut perfuming the air with new beginnings and all of the sugary sweet promise of summer. This place, this moment was clearly my chance to try and fix things.

"I'm sorry," I squeaked. "I'm sorry for jumping out of the window. I didn't know what else to do." I tossed my hands in the air. "I'm sorry for rejecting you. I don't want to, but you don't remember most of the incident in the staff room when I almost...almost killed you." We hadn't talked about that event much. On the one hand, it had been the glorious moment when our friendship blossomed into something more. On the other hand, it had been the moment I'd been dreading. The moment I'd lost control with someone I...loved. *Father Who Turned Away, have mercy*—I loved Daniel.

Was this my brain on pregnancy hormones? Or had this human with perpetual dirt under his fingernails won my heart? I should probably tell him. *No, no*. It was too soon. We weren't officially dating. I wasn't his girlfriend. I was just some fae office friend with a really good glamour and a bouncy rack. That's all.

Oh, fuck. Here it comes.

"I love you."

The words came out soft and rounded like pillows to the face.

It was Daniel's turn to blink. His expression melted. After a millennium squeezed into a milli-second, a corner of his mouth turned up. The other corner turned up. He unclicked his seatbelt then unfastened mine. His earth-worn hands collected me and lifted me over the gear-shift. Daniel settled me in his lap and pressed a lever so his chair shot back. It gave me enough room to fit between him and the steering wheel.

Daniel freed a hand and dragged the bottom of his tee-shirt to my leaking eyes. The maneuver left his sun-tanned abs exposed and pressing against me.

My glamour wavered. I looked him in his eyes as mine shifted back and forth from human blue to black sclera with silver irises. I waited for the horror. The rejection. At this close range, there was no way to hide the real me. I was too upset to hold the illusion. I wrapped my arms around him and let it fall away. My skin darkened to a dusky blue. My fingers and toes sharpened into talons. My teeth lengthened into points.

Daniel ran a hand through my inky hair.

"Stars," he whispered.

Hesitantly, I backed away enough to see his face. He saw mine.

"There are stars...in your hair." His eyes widened. His face seemed younger than it had a moment ago. Young enough to build a rocket ship in a treehouse. Innocent enough to believe gophers has stolen his Easter eggs.

I looked down at the spill of light-drinking threads.

"I am descended from Lilith, Adam's first wife." I spoke quietly into the private space between us. "She was the Night Mother."

He curled a few strands around his finger and watched the tiny heavenly bodies twinkle through the blackness.

"Are those—?"

"Constellations? Yes, I mean no. They are reflections of the night sky."

"You have galaxies in your hair?"

I wiped my eyes on his tee-shirt again, sniffed, and nodded.

He freed his other hand and cupped my face. My blue face. My face with eyes too big to make sense in his world. Teeth too sharp not to be a threat.

"So beautiful."

I felt another round of sobs rushing to the surface. He held me as they burst forth. They echoed off the cliff of the road cut. A fae's tears in a foreign land had power. He didn't know that. He didn't know a lot. How had I landed here in this Jeep with this amazing, clueless man? This was not the place for my kind. I called the rainbows to me and slowly my skin took on a human hue. My teeth rounded. My eyes blued.

"Wait." Daniel gripped my face with both his hands. "One more second." His gaze roamed over my face. My hair. My body. And then he said it.

"I love you too." My heart swelled like that furry green Christmas man—the Gench. It beat so hard in my chest I was sure my ribs were going to open a screen door and kick the muscle out like a misbehaving cat. "The real you, Lilith. All of you."

We sat in the Jeep for a long time. Listening to the birds sing, the river rush, and the ice melting in my soul.

4

OLD WORLD LILITH

100% Night Monster

It took us another hour to reach the Wildlife Management Area deep inside the West Virginia mountains and one more hour to reach our destination via a steep gravel track. Most of the trail was switchbacks. We splashed through stream crossings and bumped over boulder fields until we came to the end of the road. The rock scramble ahead of us wasn't passable, but the Jeep's all-terrain tires and snorkel had served us well.

"Welp, thanks for the ride." I grabbed my day pack and leapt out of the Jeep. I breathed in the warm scent of pine needles upon pine needles.

"What?"

"Daniel, we've been over this. I'm paying an unexpected visit to a murderous monster. You can't come with me." I kissed him on his handsome mouth and started for the scramble.

"Wait a minute. I drove all this way and I'm just supposed to turn around and leave you here in the wilderness?"

"Exactly."

"I'm not going back to Maryland without you."

"Okay, then I'll meet you for dinner at that BBQ place we passed and we can drive back together."

"The barbeque place three towns back?"

"Yep."

"Lilith, you can't fly down this mountain. There are hunters up here."

"Well, they better be loaded for bear." I loved that expression. "Are there bears in this part of the state?" I turned and sprinted up the precarious wall of tumbled rock. As soon as my hands touched the rough, broken stone a sense of peace settled over me. I'd learned as a child that my particular species was bred to survive in inhospitable places. I was a dweller in places of broken earth. According to the Talmud, Liliths were meant to live out a lonely existence in remote wastelands. Something about cracked, snake-infested ground felt right. The ancient Hebrew tome goes on to describe my ideal environment as involving wildcats, hyenas, and goat-demons. I had yet to meet any of those, but—sure—the more the merrier.

"Yes. Yes, there are bears here, Lilith, and a gentleman does not drive to the middle of nowhere and leave his girlf—someone on a mountain."

I reached the top of the rockslide and perched on a fallen tree trunk. My talons clamped onto the rotting wood, steadying me as I peered down at him. He'd said it and couldn't take it back. I was his "girlf". I'd never been anybody's girlf before. Was that pure unadulterated glee I was feeling or had I just been struck by dry lightning? The smile on my face threatened to dislocate my ears.

"I'll be fine. Take the four-wheel drive slowly on those hairpin curves. I'll see you down there."

I didn't wait for Daniel's reply. The wilderness was calling. This wasn't a wasteland though. It was a verdant mountain ridge filled with animal life, plant life, shady springs, and absolutely nothing manmade. I could see why Lilith had chosen this location. The valleys on either side provided a view of approaching threats. The land provided food; the forest supplied shelter. A Lilith could survive here for centuries unmolested. Or unmolesting. Except for the occasional hunter or hiker, this Lilith must be pretty lonely. I was gladder than glad that Daniel wasn't with me. This was no land for hot-ass archeologists in skin-tight tee-shirts.

I picked my way through the hardwoods and clambered into the thin pines that grew like stubble on the top of the ridge. The bones of the mountain jutted along the top creating dramatic cliffs and stunning overlooks. I wanted nothing more than to take a running leap off one of the monolithic slabs and fly over the hills and valleys below, but my wings were a nighttime manifestation only. I had to wait for dusk to take that flight. Plus, West Virginia was a glamour-apparent state, which meant I'd have to somehow manage to call my full Lilith form for flight while holding my glamour an inch away from my skin so that a human on-looker wouldn't be "fooled" by my evil fae magic.

I looked around. I listened. There were no humans for miles. West Virginia was an oasis of natural beauty, but until they re-thought their rules regarding the fae, I'd leave it off my vacation list.

I'd hiked to the northern edge of the ridge with a gurgling mix of excitement and anxiety in my stomach. I hadn't seen Lilith since I was a child. She'd left the Underhill abruptly before I'd reached the age of understanding. I'd always assumed she'd been granted a writ of egress allowing her to come and go the way I now did, but she had never come back. Maybe I was wrong. Maybe she'd been forced out. She *was* a Lilith and everyone knew Hamus hated our kind. Maybe he'd convinced the Council to banish her from the Faerie Lands or, at least, the Maryland Underhill.

I tried to recall her features as I walked down a narrow deer path. *Yes, we all look alike*, but I remembered a coldness to her face and a fever in her eyes. I recalled her general beauty and how I'd envied the weight of her breasts and the slope of her hips. I'd known my curves were coming, but back then my whole life had been about yearning. To be older, to be sexy, to be free. The day Lilith stepped into a portal and vanished she'd been all of those things.

We'd never really talked much. I'd been so young when she'd left. I'd learned later that it was unusual for two Liliths to reside in the same pocket of Faerie. Why that was, I still didn't know. Was it a territory thing? Would we have been in competition for the same lovers? I didn't have a problem sharing. Maybe other

Liliths didn't feel the same way. There were so few fae species strong enough to survive us, how could we not share? Had she left to give me her seat at the mana buffet? Maybe it was just that we were rare, born of tragedy, and always an orphan. There were seven Liliths in the continental US and not all of us lived in underhills.

I breathed in the fresh air and listened to the silence. I could live like this. Happily. My vision of a cabin in the wilderness vanished before I'd even started the floorplans. A wisp of home-sickness stirred low in my abdomen. Was it the child growing inside me that made me miss the Underhill? Did that giant, unknowable creature watch over Liliths the way it watched over the other fae species? I didn't have the best relationship with that underground mountain, but maybe my child would. She'd have to. She'd be on her own...like I was.

I glimpsed a clearing ahead and chose a path between two trees. I'd almost stepped through when I felt it. Fae magic. I crept close to the sigils carved in the trees. Wards. I could wait for nightfall and try and fly over the wall of energy, but that would be creepy. This wasn't an attack. I was here as a friend—associate—something. Friends announce themselves.

"Hello." I offered a greeting first in my native tongue and then in English. Nothing. "Lilith?" Something moved in the deeper green of the slope below me. I put my back to the ward and dropped into Field Agent mode. I'd brought down specimens much larger and meaner than one hermit sex fairy, but

Liliths were scrappy. Something told me this Lilith in particular didn't enjoy unannounced guests.

"Lilith." A husky female voice sifted through the trees to my left. "This is my territory."

Welp, that answered the question as to why two Liliths didn't share the same living space. I guess my plans to start a Lilith commune were flushed. Maybe a Lilith support group or at the very least a Lilith happy hour was still on the table. What about a Lilith book club—that could be totally online. No need for bloodshed or sloppy seconds.

"Hi. Yes, I am aware. I'm just here for a little information and then I'll be gone."

"You're from the Maryland Underhill." A lithe, blue body stepped from behind a stand of scrubby pines. Lilith's cool features were untouched by time, but her curves had streamlined and as she slinked toward me, I realized that she wasn't nearly as tall as I remembered.

"Yes." I smiled. "I was a child when we last spoke."

"You are still a child."

Her eyes raked me and I did a quick reassessment of my appearance. The tips of the talons jutting from my bare feet were painted a bright, tropical red. My hiking shorts and BOHO tank top were on trend in the human world, but not very fae-like. On the way up the mountain, I'd tied my hair into two high ponytails on either side of my head. The cute hairstyle kept the strands out of my eyes as I climbed, but now I wished I'd taken the ponytails out when I'd reached the top.

The Lilith standing in front of me was the wildness of wind, the racing of water, the sparkle of sun. She was what I imagined our foremothers looked like back when the earth was young and the children of Adam's first wife roamed unchallenged. Before the underhills took us in. Before humans claimed the biome. And, I noticed, she was not wearing her glamour. She was not wearing anything.

"I remember you." Her eyes finished their circuit. She'd pressed the subtotal button and I'd come up short. "You spend a lot of time with humans, I see." She waved a hand and the wards on the trees sparked and went dark. "Ladies first." Lilith swept her arm in the direction of the sunlit clearing beyond the warded trees.

With a wary, sideways glance, I passed through the entrance and stepped into the light. Lilith followed and waved her arm again. The wards sparked and cooled.

"We are safe here. You can dispose of your glamour."

"Thank you." I shook my head and wiped my hands down my arms. The rainbows on my skin peeled and floated away like spiderwebs on the breeze.

"You may remove your…disguise." She pointed to my clothing.

O—kay.

I slipped out of my shorts and pulled my tank top over my head. I left my clothes in a pile by the tree line. Lilith gave me one cold, approving nod.

"What brings you to my mountain?" Lilith asked as she turned and walked away from me. I assumed I was to follow her. So, I did.

"I—I have news from the Underhill."

I followed her across the clearing to a giant three-story boulder split into two halves. The sun licked my skin with its heated tongue as we climbed the lower outcroppings to the central cluster. I stepped over a rattlesnake coiled in the noonday rays. His diamond-patterned body had formed a tiny volcano of warmth. An eagle perched on the branch of a dead tree poking from the base of the split stone. It swiveled its white head and regarded me with its yellow predatory eye.

We stepped into the cool shadows collected in the fecund space shaped by the twin obelisks. The open-air chamber was no more than ten feet across, but hid natural chambers inside its grassy domain. A set of piled stones shaped a staircase winding along two of its walls. We climbed to the top of the stairs and the mountain range opened up before us. Misty valleys, winding rivers, emerald green mountains rolled away in every direction. My breath caught in my throat. Was this the throne of the Father Who Turned Away? My knees tingled with the impulse to kneel. Surely, this was where all prayers drifted up to?

"Welcome to my home." Lilith gestured to the sweeping expanse. "Please sit." She settled on a rocky ledge and folded her lean legs beneath her.

I did the same. The stone ledge was warm and smooth and sized for a god.

"The Underhill is of no concern to me." She turned away from me and said it to the air, to the sunlight, but not to me.

"That's a good thing because it's closed."

"Closed?" She turned back to me, pupils widening.

"Sealed off. No one can get in or out."

"Has the Underhill deemed you unworthy?"

"Oh, I'm sure it has, but it's not just me that can't get back in. No one can. There are no portals and no communication between realms."

Her smooth brow crinkled.

"The last message I received was from the Council of Elders warning me to stay away. That was weeks ago."

Something dark slid across Lilith's silver eyes. "So, they are trapped."

"It would appear."

Lilith turned back to the breathtaking view. Had the older fae gotten used to it? Was this vista something she barely noticed anymore. Her gaze seemed far away, past the mountains, past the horizon.

"The only other contact I have received was a very brief fire missive from Hamus, King of the Fire Drakes. It didn't make a lot of sense, but it was urgent. It's why I'm here."

"Hmph. And what did the demon's missive say?" Her voice held a chill to it.

"*Bring the Swamp Witch* and he instructed me to hurry."

A slow dagger of a thought carved a smile on my host's face. A sound much like a giggle erupted from the wild woman. It cooled my blood. I suddenly had the urge to slide out of arm's reach.

"You'll never find the witch." Lilith almost sang it.

"You know who she is?"

"Of course I do. I've lived on this continent a long time, child."

"Where can I find her?"

"Why should I help you? Or more to the point—why should I help them?" The smile fell from her dusky face. I knew it was pointless trying to pick out the signs of age on an Old World fae, but I could feel her years hanging in the air like a lead balloon. She looked tired. She'd been dragging some ancient resentment around for so long that it had changed her, dimmed her, hardened her. I could only guess at what it was, but my guess wouldn't be far from the mark. Liliths were both vital and reviled. Desired and disdained. None of us were treated well.

"There are good people trapped in the Underhill as well." I thought of my brilliant bestie Daphne, Hennig the Hilarious as I liked to call him, and Gillian—the shyest of my co-workers, but possessing a heart of gold. I had friends throughout the underground mountain who clearly hadn't moved quickly enough when the Council called for an evacuation. *Yes, I have more than three fae friends. Don't look so surprised.* Anyway, I had no idea what condition they were in. Were they safe and just hunkered down while the Underhill went through another colossal mood swing? Or was it worse? There were stories of underhills rejecting their fae inhabitants, violently expelling them, or worse...digesting them.

"Please. I can tell there is bad blood between you and the Council. Trust me, I'm not trying to save *them*, but my best friend is locked in there. If this Swamp Witch can help, I need to find her."

Lilith unfolded me with her gaze and studied me like a map. I had no idea what she was looking for, but I sure hoped I had it. Unless it was a red flag in which case I hoped I didn't have it.

I waited and tried not to fidget while she deliberated.

"It's possible that they have taken the inner roads and migrated to another underhill."

I nodded. It was possible, but if the portals to the human universe were sealed, I had to assume the portals to other fae pocket universes, known as the *Ways*, were closed too.

"Or the Council has gotten them all killed."

Fuck. I guessed that was a reasonable possibility too. Petros, the weeping twin of Cephas Stonefist had mentioned something about the Underhill just before I'd been sent out on vacation, but I couldn't recall his words. Had the Council done something to piss the Underhill off?

"Maybe you're right. I don't know. All I do know is that I have to at least try to help."

"Why do you care?" She peered closely at my map. "You are a Lilith. Made in the Night Mother's image. You are above them. And yet, they look down on you." She leaned close enough for me to see the starlight in her wild hair. It sparkled with the same constellations as mine. It drank the sunshine the same way mine did. She was like me.

A wave of longing washed over me and my hand went to my abdomen.

Her silver eyes followed.

I longed for things I'd never had. I longed for kinship…family.

"You are with child." It was more a statement than a question and whispered like the most sacred of invocations.

I nodded.

I watched a primordial ocean of grief wash over her. The weight of our species' curse settled over us both like the shadow of a passing cloud. In that moment, I wanted nothing more than to touch her. Not in a sexual way. In a comforting way. In a way fae rarely touched.

"I am sorry for you." The words surprised me. They wobbled from her lips as if they weren't the words she'd meant to say. "May I touch?"

My heart leapt.

I leaned back exposing my mid-section, laying myself bare for the world on this high throne.

Her fingertips settled on my skin so lightly. Talons touched, but didn't press. At last, her cool palm flattened against my womb. The sensation thrilled through me like no other touch I'd ever experienced before. Tears welled in the corners of my eyes. I wished I could share this moment with my mother.

She closed her own eyes as if she could feel the swishing tail of my emotion. She opened them and we looked into each other.

Her lips formed a word, but I could barely hear past the music in my heart.

"Twins." The sound finally penetrated my hazy head.

"What?"

"Father Who Turned Away," she whispered as she adjusted her hand and looked into the distance.

"No...triplets."

The world spun.

5

TIMBER RATTLESNAKE

100% Pit Viper

Her gaze returned to mine but she was still focused on a distant place.

"Maybe more."

"M—more? I—I have more?" I was surrounded by air, but somehow, I couldn't force any of it into my lungs.

Reality shifted again. I'd prepared myself for the next ten months of life with my new occupant. I'd accepted her into my heart. My soul. I'd circled the wagons around us in my head. I needed more wagons.

"H—" *Silly me*—I almost asked how. How could this happen, but I knew. I remembered the pinching in my side as the Immortal Serpent brought my eggs to bear in my womb. He'd called on the great reserves of mana existing inside his deathless body to bring forth extra life. How many eggs did he release through my fallopian tubes? How many had he fertilized when he'd filled me to overflowing with his monstrous jets of cum?

"Are you sure?"

"Every Lilith has a gift." She said it like I should have known that. "Mine is the gift to see what is hidden."

"I—I don't think I have a gift." *It figures.* I was the only Lilith without something special. Unless a gorgeous rack is considered a gift.

"Can I bear that many children?"

"A Lilith's body is very accommodating."

Yes, it was, but Gods, what kind of child birth was I looking at? Would I spend my last hours of existence in horrible pain? Was it harder or easier to bear naga babies? If a Lilith had a male child, he would resemble the father almost completely. If a Lilith had a female child, she was basically a complete genetic copy of the mother. Could my body hold an array of fae children? Could my heart?

I got the answer to my last question immediately. Like the Christmas Gench, my heart was swelling to fit my off-spring...my family. I leaned forward as my tears rained down on the god-sized altar of rock. Wasted magic, but not wasted emotion. I'd shower my children with love for as long as I drew breath.

Lilith's hand slipped from my body, but the enchantment of her touch lingered. The sublime memory of Daniel's embrace clung to me as well. If I never made it back into the Underhill, I could survive out here in the human world, powered by touch and the tiny stirrings inside my womb.

"Are these your first children?"

I nodded, overcome and reeling from this new reality.

"Watch carefully for their first breathes. That is when you must dispatch them."

"What?"

"The curse acts quickly if you do not." Her voice had armor. Despite my horror, it didn't feel like she was trying to hurt me. If anything, it felt like she was trying to help.

I shook my head numbly at the thought of doing harm to my children. The ancient human scrolls described Liliths as, among other things, baby killers, but that wasn't our true nature. That was what the Father Who Turned Away had made of us.

"Child." That one word revealed the ocean of time between our ages. "You do not understand what you would be giving up. You can not let the Father Who Turned Away win."

If I killed my offspring according to his mandate, wouldn't that be the win for him?

Was my head spinning or was it just the planet rotating below us and we were high enough to feel it? I'd come for advice and I'd gotten it—just not on the subject I wanted.

"Who is the Swamp Witch?" I slammed the door shut on the topic of babies.

Lilith blinked at me. She folded my map in her mind. Withdrew her interest. Walls went up as tall as the boulder we now sat on.

"It doesn't matter. She will never reveal herself to you."

"I can be pretty convincing." I held her steely gaze.

"You already know her and, trust me, you've already made a bad impression."

"I've met her?"

"Yes."

"When? Where?"

"If I tell you, you must promise me something."

Hmm, if I wasn't on-guard before, I was now. Promises were a distinctly unfae-like concept. For someone steeped in the old ways, why would she ask such a human thing of me?

"A promise?" I asked.

"An intention," she clarified.

"I will tell you where to find the Witch if you will give your situation the necessary consideration. There is chaos in you, but you are not thantos. Murdering innocents will be hard for you. But once the deed is done, there are ways to prevent you from ever being in this situation again. You are a rare wonder. You grace this world with your presence. Your *living* presence."

I'd never had anyone speak to me like that. I'd received a few compliments in college and my roommate, Dalia, was a fountain of flattery, but no fae had ever sung my praises in that way.

I nodded numbly as the words sank beneath my skin. She knew there would be no verbal contract between us, but she seemed to accept my acknowledgement.

"The Swamp Witch was present when you stole the young male dryad from the Great Dismal. The dryads and naiads of the coastal swamp are her charges. She maintains their habitat as part of the deal her ancestors made with the land for sanctuary from the slave-traders long ago. You are—how do the humans say—public enemy number one." She giggled like a sinister windchime.

Crap.

Of all the swamps, it had to be that one.

"This won't be easy."

She didn't hide her amusement at my predicament. I was beginning to think of her as a quirky aunt with pointy teeth and a bad sense of humor. The type of relative who showed up to human gatherings with a bottle of booze and unwanted advice. Even so, if I were human, I'd relish my time with her. I'd even thought about lingering there with her on that sun-warmed rock at the edge of the world. That all changed when the wind shifted and the hot, musky smell of human male enveloped us.

"Daniel." I'd barely uttered his name before Lilith was up and jumping over the cluster of boulders.

Son of a bitch. He'd followed me.

Lilith's taloned feet gauged the grass as she hit the clearing at a run. I leapt down behind her.

"No," I shouted, but Lilith's eros spilled from her lithe form as she ran leaving a ribbon of desire in the air. She was genus Venereae and already lost to her impulse. I'd had practice over the last few weeks ignoring Daniel's delectable man scent. With that said, the pulse of my heart as I ran, the sweet tang of Lilith's eros, the soft slide of air on my bare body—it was all too much. My eros rose.

"Lilith, don't," I shouted, but I might as well have spoken in another language. I saw how her lean muscles flexed, how her shoulders bunched with the need to fly, how her depthless black hair whipped and curled like a living thing. *This is what a true Lilith looks like.* The thought invaded my mind like a blinding blade of truth. I reached for her midnight locks to slow her even as I marveled at her perfection.

My fingers caught enough of the serpentine strands to get a grip. I yanked her head back as she dove for the tree-line. I caught a quick movement from the corner of my eye.

"Don't run," I ordered Daniel. He was several yards into the trees, but we were already too close. "Stay still." He froze.

Lilith hissed and threw a pointy elbow at my temple. The impact stunned me. I lost my grip on her, and she lunged forward.

"He is mine," I screamed like the night creature I was.

Lilith slowed, but she'd already made it to the warded trees. She waved her hand and the sigils flared. I caught up to her and slipped my arm around her neck.

She hissed as I squeezed.

Daniel took a step back, but her hand shot out and gripped him by his windpipe.

"Then, we will share him," she gurgled and dropped her weight. I somersaulted over her. By the time I righted myself, Lilith had Daniel hugged against her. "Thank you for this delicious gift." She licked his face like a lollipop and Daniel's body spasmed. Eros—that sweet, invisible elixir—flowed over him. His face went slack as her hands unwrapped him like a giant piece of candy. His shirt tore. His jeans peeled away.

That was my piece of candy.

So hard. So ready to be sucked.

"Give him to me."

My super-charged eros flooded the clearing drowning us all.

"As soon as I'm done." Her hands slid through his hair, down his body. Her lips covered his.

Daniel moaned.

"That's a good little human. Submit to me and I will give you your heart's desire."

Daniel's eyes shifted drunkenly to me. Lilith grabbed his jaw and turned his gaze back to her. "Tell me what you dream of at night when you are alone and aching with desire?"

Lilith's taloned hands made their way to his thighs. Deft fingers found his straining cock.

Daniel cried out.

"He. Is. Mine." I bit her. I actually bit her. Blood teased across my tongue. So sweet. So fulfilling.

Lilith shrieked.

Without thinking, I fastened my mouth over the bite mark and sucked. Coppery bliss filled my mouth. Lilith tipped her head back in ecstasy. I lifted my mouth and her face rolled toward me. Her silvery eyes flashed as her tongue slicked across my dripping lips.

My breath caught. I crushed my mouth against hers. I jammed my tongue between her lips, past her pointed teeth. I tasted her. Invaded her.

She bit down on my tongue and hot blood flooded both our mouths. Rapturous pain tickled through me, sharpening my nipples, clenching my inner muscles. There was no coming back from this.

Lilith released Daniel and his slack body fell to the ground. She reached for me.

"So much power," she breathed into my ear. I'd wondered what it would be like to have another Lilith's attentions. I cried out as she lowered her mouth to my breasts. Her tongue teased like no other. It rubbed my beaded flesh until the roof of my mouth tingled. Her hands massaged my round, supple flesh. She locked her mouth over my swollen tips and sucked at the great well of mana trapped inside me. I gasped as she fed on my life force, so exquisitely draining.

"Lilith," Daniel breathed. He struggled to lift his head. He forced himself to his elbows, still naked and prone in the warm grass. Lilith's head turned. With a slippery wet sound, her lips released my flesh. Wisps of energy trailed between my breasts and her tongue. I was left weak and warm and shivering with need.

"Do you want us to play with you, Little Toy?"

Daniel's face reflected a month worth of pent-up desire. All the weeks of keeping our hands to ourselves, all the days we hadn't kissed, the nights of lingered goodnight hugs and unfulfilled dreams rushed to the surface of his skin. He glowed with yearning.

"Yes." His husky answer unraveled me.

Lilith dropped to all fours and crawled to him. She inhaled his scent, his pumping life force. She settled over him and licked him like spilled ice cream. I watched as he thrilled at the sensation. Threads of his energy rode her tongue.

She pinned his strong arms as she nipped and laved his chest, his stomach. Daniel's face contorted into a mask of carnal delight. She released his arms and grasped his powerful thighs.

My heart sped up as she forced his legs apart. She buried her shadowy blue face in his warm male scent. Rolled his delicate sac on her wide tongue. She probed him, consuming every fragrant piece of his sun-drenched body.

"Please," he begged in a voice cracked with hunger.

"Do you want me to worship your manhood?" She spoke over his hardened flesh like it was a microphone. His turgid column strained toward the sky.

"Yes."

Lilith grinned darkly. Her tongue darted for the bead of liquid clinging to his swollen head, recoiling at the last second.

"Do you want me to suck you until there is nothing left?"

"Yes!"

Her tongue shot out and captured the transparent drop of fluid.

Daniel cried out at the graze of her moist tongue. Lilith's pupils swelled. My knees buckled.

"Don't." My protest was barely a whisper. "You'll kill him."

Lilith grinned in a way that revealed every sharpened tooth in her mouth. Instead of lowering her lips over his rigid cock, her hands stole under his body, gripped him by his glutes and thrust his engorged staff into her salivating mouth. She held still as a breezeless night, eyes fixed on his rapturous face as she pumped him in and out of her drooling mouth.

Daniel gasped for breath as her tongue slid past her lips licking and sucking him at the same time. She varied her movements, sucking, swallowing, twisting. The delicious sound of her frothing mouth nursing his flesh spread moisture between my legs. I fell to my hands and knees and tore at the ground with my talons.

"You have to stop." But I knew she wouldn't. Couldn't. Eros saturated her brain and all she knew now was pleasure. Greedy, grasping, devouring gratification. I had to summon the strength to separate her from Daniel, but I dared not touch him. My body demanded that I join them. I wanted to relish his ecstasy, luxuriate in her hedonistic joy. I wanted to fuck them both at the same time. Over and over until the mountain we kneeled on turned to sand.

Daniel shouted to the sky as he exploded in her mouth. Lilith drank every drop of him. The world spun. His lungs filled with air. Once, twice, and she called to his softening flesh. Daniel's body quaked as his column hardened again. It purpled under her touch, swelling to a size his skin could barely contain.

"That's a good Little Toy. Time to give me what I want." Lilith rose to her knees and straddled his hips.

"Oh, God." Daniel shook under the weight of her inhuman desire. A Lilith's cravings were too much for a mortal nervous system.

"Tell me you want me," she cooed as she hovered over his swollen cock. She was wonderous in the noonday light. Cornflower blue skin stretched over wild, free-range muscles. Martini glass breasts tipped with stiff sapphire nipples, long, graceful neck, plump, pillowy lips, streamlined nose, knife bright eyes, arched onyx brows, and hair a curtain of darkest night. Her image dwelled in the hind brains of every child of Adam. Every spawn of the Night Mother dreamed, wished, secretly yearned for that glorious being to visit them in their beds.

I shook with need. I hovered on the edge of a disastrous decision. I loved him. I'd hoped for a life with him. I'd fooled myself into thinking we'd find a way.

"Tell me you want me," she repeated, slowly lowering the petals of her slick flesh over the drooling head of his cock. No creature could resist her. Not now. Not at the dancing edge of such rhapsody.

Daniel's gaze found mine.

"I want you."

It was all I could take. I loved him. I needed him and he needed me. The decision was made for me. I crawled to him. Lifted his head. Kissed him with everything I had.

"Daniel's mouth released from mine in a cry of delight. Lilith lowered her eager body onto his. I looked up to see his straining cock buried in the slick bloom of her devouring flesh. I held him, kissed him, protected him as Lilith rode him up the long hill of her hunger. His breath was unsteady, but his eyes were filled with presence. How was he doing this? How was he surviving?

His gaze found mine again as his body bucked with her thrusts. I tried to be with him for his last moments. The petals of Lilith's venereae anatomy had unfurled, had latched on to him to drink his life force to the last drop.

"Stay with me," he whispered.

"I'm here."

"Share this with me." He forced the words out around a deep, uncontrolled moan.

I shook my head.

"Please."

I covered his mouth with mine trying to trap his wish with my lips. "Please," he begged. My tongue devoured the soft supplication. A thin tendril of mana drifted from his mouth to mine. I'd literally just eaten a piece of him.

Daniel smiled as if he'd felt the exchange, as if he was aware of all that was happening to him.

"Let me taste you." His request held a hint of the manly confidence I found so hard to resist.

"Daniel, I don't think you understand what you're asking for." He must have been delirious. Strangely, he didn't look like a man whose life was slipping away. He looked like a human overcome and laying himself bare.

"I know what I'm asking. I'm asking you to sit on my face and let me give you what I've wanted to give you for so long."

My jaw dropped. My skin flushed so fast I thought the sun had picked our mountain on which to focus all its rays.

"Trust me, Lil. I can take it."

I had no idea how he was still breathing in and out much less asking to tend to my pleasure.

"For me." He flashed a loose version of his Daniel smile. The one that melted my heart and dampened my undies.

Before I knew it, I was throwing my leg over him. I scooped his silky hair out of the way and walked my knees up until I straddled his face.

"Beautiful," he whispered as he got his first look at a Lilith's genitals. The first layer of my labia had already opened for him revealing my inner petals and the peak which had already swollen with just the idea of his tongue on it. "So, beautiful."

Behind me, Lilith moaned. The sight of my curvy ass hovering over Daniel's hungry face must have been fuel for her ravenous fire. I know it would have been for mine. His body jerked forward at a faster pace as the succubus found the new rhythm she wanted. Her breath was heavy on the air.

I lower myself until I could feel the stubble bristling his upper lip and chin. His mouth opened and a dream came out. Slick, squirming, searching my every corner. Thick and rubbing, then thin and teasing.

"Lesser Gods!" My eros flooded every cell of my body. I inhaled it like a drug. My brain fizzed. Lilith cried out. Daniel made a strangled sound. "Are you okay?" I sat up and checked his face for signs of life.

He nodded, took a few deep breaths, then gripped my thighs and forced me down to his waiting tongue. I moaned as he probed me. He sucked my slick petals into his mouth and nibbled. He called all the blood in my body to him. I arched my back as he flattened his tongue against me. He rolled and pressed, inviting me to show him what I wanted, where I wanted it.

I rested my hands on my thighs and swiveled my hips as he teased around my swollen mound. I reveled in the quick darting nudges he offered as my body began to rock. All fear, all my concerns fell away as Daniel worshipped my soaking wet crevice, as he merged with my flesh, matching my rhythm. He flicked my aching bud with the tip of his tongue. I cried out. My voice rode the breeze in waves of wordless moans and gasps.

I rocked. He dragged. I moaned. He flicked. Pressure built in my chest, in my groin. I was climbing the hill.

"Daniel." I spoke his name like a prayer. Eros poured over us.

He gasped and sped up his rhythm. He was climbing the hill too.

"Yes, baby." I let him know he'd found the right pressure in the right place at the right time. "Just like that." His body bucked under the weight of two succubi writhing their way to ecstasy. "Yes, my love. Don't stop." My legs began to shake. A sweet ache spread through my abdomen. It leaked into my muscles, my veins. "That's it. Please. Give it to me, baby." He licked me hard and fast. I bucked as my muscles pushed me to the top of the hill. "Harder," I begged and he complied. He dragged his tongue across my peak once, twice, and I burst on his third delicious pass. Mana exploded from me bathing the mountain top.

Daniel's body seized.

Rapture tore from Lilith's throat.

We spasmed together.

A vast, cracked desert burned beneath my feet. Hills with scant vegetation rose in the distance, offering shade for only the smallest of prey. It was pointless to go in that direction. For the third time in as many days, my gaze turned to the rising sun. To the land of men. Where noise and light and wonders dazzled the eye. It was a forbidden place, but it sheltered the biggest prey.

I was starting to believe that the Father might be turning away from us, instead, focusing his eye on Eve's children. Were our sins so large that he would let us starve as punishment?

I would not starve.

I would gorge myself on the flesh of men and take my place above them.

6

BUZZARD

100% Turkey Vulture

I woke to the sight of two black birds wheeling above. Their wings were spread wide to catch the fickle drafts blowing up and over the craggy mountain top. *Cathartes aura* or Turkey Vultures, better known as Buzzards. They had an awesome defense mechanism. If a bird or animal or human got too close, the vultures could vomit on them at will.

Were they circling me?

Oh, shit. Was I dead?

Daniel. Was Daniel dead?

I sat up and gripped my pounding head.

"Daniel?"

I turned toward the sound of a rhythmic huffing to see Daniel lying motionless on the sun-warmed grass and Lilith applying chest compressions.

"What?" I coughed as I realized my own heart wasn't beating as it should. Mixed into the *wah-wumps* were a few *wah-wah-wumps*. That wasn't right.

I scrambled to my feet and stumbled to Daniel's side. I lifted his neck, pinched his nose, closed my mouth over his and breathed a few rescue breaths into him. His chest rose and fell. He coughed into my mouth.

"What happened?" My head wobbled in Lilith's direction.

"Everybody died."

"What?" Daniel and I asked at the same time, but Daniel's voice was barely a whisper.

"Well, I don't know if I actually died. I might have just passed out, but you and you definitely died." Her sharp, blue finger pointed at me then Daniel. "After a few seconds, you started breathing on your own, but this guy was a goner."

"You saved me?" His hand went to his chest. His fingers weakly gripped the fossil necklace glued to the top of his sternum with sweat. It seemed to be a rote action Daniel took whenever he needed to center himself.

"You're welcome." She stood and brushed the dirt from her hands. "Now, get off my mountain."

I gave her a disbelieving look.

Everything had been fine a second ago. She got hers, we got ours. I guess there'd be no snuggling for us.

But had everything been fine? Had I really died? One second, I was having a truly epic orgasm, and the next, I was standing in a desert trying to decide if I should eat a human.

"What was that about?" I must have asked the question out loud because Lilith turned on her heel and stretched her arms out to her sides.

"Good sex. That's what that was about. You need to have more fae sex, Lilith. And stop hanging around with humans. Particularly, thieves like him."

Thieves?

Daniel gave me a wary look, then tried to push to his elbows. He failed.

I looked around. What had Daniel stolen?

I pushed to my feet again, this time with less stumbling, and made my way to my clothes. I stepped into my shorts and pulled my tank top on, then, pulled Daniel's jeans up from where they'd bunched at his ankles. His shirt was badly torn, but I sat him up and helped him put it on anyway.

"Can you stand?"

He rolled onto his knees then fell face first into the grass.

"No-ff."

I took that as a "nope."

I rolled him over and stood like the Colossus of Rhodes above him.

"What did you steal?"

"Nothing."

Lilith stopped in her tracks.

"Try and remove his necklace."

I squinted at her through the sunlight.

"His necklace." She pointed. "Try to take it off him."

Daniel raised a weak palm to me. I knocked it out of the way and gripped the fossil. The miniature, spiraling horn sat in my hand like the stone it had become over millions of years. I yanked the chain, but it did not break free. I grasped the chain with both hands and tried to lift it over his messy hair, but it clung to him like a magnet.

"Daniel?" I regarded the man I'd given my heart to. Had he been keeping secrets from me? "What have you done?"

"I didn't steal it." He ripped the talisman from my hand. "I found it."

"Where?"

"At a site in Montana." His ocean eyes swam with things I didn't know. Things he had not shared.

"Which site?"

"I can't say."

"What do you mean you can't say?"

"I'm not allowed. The government has deemed it beyond top secret."

"Your government?" Lilith turned to face us across the clearing. "I want nothing to do with governments—human or fae." She pointed to the trees with their sleeping sigils. "Go. Do not disturb my sanctuary again." Her eyes flashed like lightning.

I picked Daniel up and threw him over my shoulder. He was larger and heavier than me which made for an awkward walk downhill, but I couldn't leave him on a mountain top with an angry chaos fae.

After a few minutes of blood rushing to his head, Daniel's protests stopped and he slept. When we finally arrived at the rock scramble just above where we'd left the Jeep, I thought about tossing him down it. How could he keep such a secret from me. I've told him everything. *Hmm*. Well, not everything. He knew I worked for a genetics program that was attempting to breed the fae back into existence, but I had not shared my fears regarding the Council's other plans. Plans that involved the human realm. Plans I'd only heard bits and pieces of.

"Put me down." Daniel patted my back and began to squirm. I had no choice but to spill him onto a boulder at the top of the rock field. "I think I blacked out," he slurred.

"How did you survive that experience at all?" I found a slab to sit on and crossed my arms over my chest.

Daniel heaved a sigh. The effort seemed to make him dizzy.

"The artifact." He reached for the thin fossilized spiral. I studied it as he rubbed his fingers over it. The tiny coil had chambers filled with a hard amber-like substance.

"So—what? This thing gives you some immunity to fae influence?"

"Not some—a lot, Lilith. I tried to tell you before you jumped out the window last night. It's a way for us to be together." His pirate ship gaze glittered with hope, but his face was ashen and his breathing labored.

"I don't think this talisman is as strong as you think it is. And why did you wait until last night to try and tell me? We've been together for weeks. You've been wearing that thing for a month."

It clearly wasn't the response Daniel had been hoping to hear. He sprawled over the boulder and looked up at the sky.

I used the moment of silence to leaf through all the emotions I was feeling: anger about Daniel keeping a secret, lingering bliss over the portion of sexual gratification I'd finally gotten to enjoy with him, and the tiniest sliver of hope. Was he right? Was the small, immovable relic around his neck the answer to our unspoken prayers? Was I about to spend the last months of my life with everything I'd ever wanted?

The thought knocked me back a step.

After a lengthy pause, Daniel dragged himself to his feet and started climbing down the scramble.

"Let me help you."

"I got it."

His foot slipped and he tumbled over a segment of boulders that should have taken several careful minutes to descend. I leapt down and tried to help him to his feet. He yanked his arm from my grip. I watched as he struggled down the rest of the rock field scraped and bloody.

I met him at the bottom and pulled his water bottle from the center consol. I handed it to him. He took it grudgingly and drank deeply.

"At least let me drive us off the mountain."

Daniel gave me a withering look, but he handed over the keys. That's all that mattered.

We bumped and swerved back down the switchbacks without speaking a word. I knew what needed to happen, but Daniel might never forgive me if I did it.

Decisions, decisions.

In the end, my inner chaos flipped a coin.

Heads—I drive us home, forget about the Swamp Witch, and enjoy ten months of happiness with the human I couldn't get enough of.

Tails—I dump him at the first sign of civilization, steal his Jeep, and head for the swampy coastline.

The mental coin landed on tails.

7

SPARRED OWL

*Y*es, I abandoned him and took off with his vehicle, but in my defense, I left him in the examining room of a medical center with his wallet, his water bottle, and a Snickers bar. Not the small, single serving kind, the big one for sharing. I'd excused myself, told him I'd be right back, then drove off.

What? Do you still not get that I'm a monster? I may look human, but I'm not. I'll admit—I'm a little conflicted, but sometimes the hard decisions have to be made. Daniel was in no condition to deal with an angry Lilith, much less an entire copse of pissed off dryads.

Actually, I wasn't sure if I was ready to deal with the dryads either, but it was too late to turn back now. I'd already burned four hours driving east to the Great Dismal Swamp and another hour hiking through squelching underbrush. I had to admit the snake-infested canals and bramble-covered hummocks were *right up my alley,* as you people like to say. If it weren't for the grudge-holding tree people living at its center, this wildlife refuge would be a perfect weekend getaway for me.

The sun had relinquished its throne in the buzzing sky, but dusk lingered like a lover who wanted one last smooch, and then one for the road, and one to grow on. *Enough already. Just set.* I had to wait thirty more minutes before night truly fell and I could assume my owl form. There was absolutely no chance of humans being this far into the bush and definitely not after dark so I unfurled my wings, shook my feathers out, and took to the air. I was joined by about nine million mosquitos but they didn't seem to care for fae blood.

From the air, the thickly forested Great Dismal was a shadowy green dream with a dark blue mirror at its center. Lake Drummond was the giant navel on the dismembered torso of the surviving swampland. Its virgin waters held no boats. It was rimmed by no structures. Its waters met the trees with no prelude of beaches. It was a vast bowl of warm, shallow water belonging only to the animals of the swamp...and the trees.

I gave the water a quick pass, then concentrated on the northern edge of the lake. The evening air filled with the whooping monkey calls of barred owls and the deep-throated jaw harp twangs of bull frogs. Every now and then, I caught sight of balding roads which cut oddly straight lines through the vegetation alongside narrow ditches filled with tea-colored water. Nothing that lived inside that lush wilderness walked a straight line so the roads seemed woefully out of place. Nonetheless, the narrow paths fought the encroaching flora for every rutted inch of territory. Some trails had lost the battle and died a green death, while others clung close to the amber waterways earning their keep as sunning spots for turtles and other cold-blooded denizens.

I flew in low circles over the swamp, looking for inconsistencies: a bit of strange topography, a flash of movement against the breeze. I saw nothing but a lone hybridized Sparred Owl swooping through the trees. It had the size of a Barred Owl, but the markings of a Spotted Owl. I studied the kindred spirit as it honed in on its rodent prey. But, that's the thing about hyper-focusing—even an owl could miss something. Something fast. I felt the tug before my brain even registered the delicate tendril coiled around my leg. My feet could snap a medium-sized tree in half, but a soft, green, flexible vine seemed to be my downfall—literally.

Fear pricked at my skin as I sank through the air. I tugged and bit at the tightening green thread. Thrashing didn't help. My low body weight worked against me as my wings pounded at the thick swamp air. Fear swelled to panic.

Down I went into the soupy canopy. Shivering limbs closed around me. Bark buckled. Branches cracked. I crashed to the soggy ground as more probing, green runners wrapped around me. In the space of a breath, I was cocooned by tight, wriggling ropes.

The low moan of bending wood rumbled in my chest like thunder. The still lake water behind me carried the sound out like gossip for the rest of the swamp. *The night monster has been caught. The great abductor is captured.* Giant gulps of mud sucked and burped in all directions. The dryads were coming.

Stay calm.

I ceased my struggling and closed my eyes to the shower of tiny twigs and branches raining down on me. My body heaved as roots rearranged in the wet earth beneath me. After what felt like an eternity, the swamp stilled. From a safe distance, the chorus of life carried on their chittering and groaning, but inside the dark hammock of thick trunks in which I'd been snared, silence ruled.

Patience, I reminded myself. *Trees have their own sense of time.*

Fireflies blinked. Stars danced. Fog gathered over the marshy ground carrying a thick scent of cabbage with a hint of rotting things. I held perfectly still on the spongy earth and tried not to nip at the squeezing tendrils as the forest deliberated above me. At first glance, it was hard to tell the dryads from the old growth trees. Both were wide-bodied with roots like leviathan tentacles, but when the conversation was done and the dryads opened their eyes, the living wood flowed around the other vegetation like ooze. A tall, regal cedar slurped into the hammock crowding out the smaller, slower trees. The deep crevasses of its eyes glowed with a hidden, slow-burning fire. Steam drifted from its jagged mouth as it peered down at me. Judging. The imposing tree moved close, towering over me. I examined its scaly, fissured bark, its large, barrel-shaped cones. The cedar's broad, level branches splayed to hold back the throng of curious saplings. It had an air of leadership, but that crackling glow emanating from its bowels smelled of thantos. I knew destructive energy when I caught a whiff of it. That dryad was dying.

Next to it, a scrubby pine kept pace. The smaller, hunched tree came to a stop and leaned against its taller companion resting its knobby, rheumatic joints. Its needles bristled as it glared at me through its spindly branches.

A pair of twin oaks shoved onto the small rise of land next to me. Their high, tightly grasping arms held the two entities together to create one tree with two coldly appraising faces. Were they afraid I might steal one of them like I had the willow a couple of months ago? Their swamp gas green eyes shifted as something moved toward me from behind.

I tipped my head back and swallowed loudly as the ghostly cypress glided along the water's edge. Its spidery roots fused into a skirt of rippling white wood. The effect mimicked that of a humanoid female wearing a wet, clinging gown. A wedding gown, perhaps. Every sinuous curve and valley of her hips and womanhood stood out in exquisite relief. Her narrow waist stretched high into a soft, tapered trunk. The sleek wood swelled into two pale, teardrop breasts. Delicate shoulders sprouted sturdy moss-covered branches. The appendages reached like arms ready to embrace, but I knew it wasn't a hug that tree wanted to give me. I remembered her. I recalled her anguish as my team of extractors ripped her mate from those same branching arms. Two lightning strike eyes looked down on me from a long, gaunt face. The pale embers of her trauma still glowed inside the blackened slits. Her tormented face still cried tears of blood red sap.

I deserved that look.

At least, she had him back now safe and sound.

I searched the girdle of land that flowed into the stumpy, brackish water for the tree I'd stolen. Seven weeks ago, my team and I had found the unsuspecting wooden rarity kneeling next to the lake lost in thought or whatever cogitation occupied trees. Reports of a male willow of breeding age had sent our department into a frenzy. Just about every collector in the program had joined in on that capture. Male dryads of any ilk were uncommon and damn near a breeding miracle, but a willow of the same genus and species as Daphne was a gift from the gods. *I know, I know. Satyrs are the natural male mates to the almost exclusively female dryads, but you helpful humans killed off the last of them centuries ago, soooo. Yep, we took him. By force.*

I'm sure he wouldn't be happy to see me. We'd stolen him from his home and turned him into a fuck toy until he'd accomplished the goal of impregnating my esteemed colleague and bestie. Daphne hadn't exactly been thrilled about the hook up either, but when the Council of Elders says fuck, you ask how high?

From the looks of it, his mate was even less thrilled to see me. I had a lot to say, but the dryad standing as still as death in the shallow water of Lake Drummond had the right to speak first. So, I waited. And waited. The trees were silent so long that the owls and frogs resumed their songs inside the hammock. I held my tongue as long as I could. I really did, but time was wasting so I snapped the larger, wooden vines and pushed to my feet. More vines ensnared me.

"Listen, I'm sorry—"

A spear of pale wood shot toward me so fast, I barely had time to shift my weight. The lance caught me in the side nearly impaling me. I stumbled backward until my back touched warm, rough bark. The cypress dryad's spikey root pinned me against the twin oaks. They seemed all too willing to be the skin-shredding backboard of my demise. Their leaf-tipped fingers reached down to hold me in place. My talons ached to break the wooden skewer. My teeth yearned to shred those crooked fingers, but I held off. I endured the pain. Clearly, the bolt wasn't meant to kill me.

"You do not speak," the dryad's voice rang hollow and stank of mildew. Her roots climbed the thin bank leaving her half in and half out of the water. She leaned over the small rise of land until her face hovered just above mine. "You have no voice here."

I heaved a sigh which pulled at my side and reminded me I was not alone in my skin. The sharp javelin pushed a little deeper. My flesh tore. I'd come here prepared to donate a little blood to the cause, but not my children's blood.

I was starting to lose my patience.

"Kll hr nd snd hr skuuull bck to th faaae," the stunted, little pine rasped. Her sappy syllables stuck together giving her a heck of a speech impediment. The effect was more than a little creepy. I assumed her gender only because dryads were mostly female.

"Then, we will never know his fate," the massive cedar rumbled. Another female. Her words were ashy and smelled of burning peat.

"Use her to bargain," the left side of the conjoined oak offered.

"An exchange," the right side added. Sisters? Or mates?

"What excha—" I began, but was cut off by a jolt of pain from the sharpening javelin piercing my hip.

I assumed the verbal speech was for my benefit, but no one was speaking to me. The smaller trees huddling behind the dryads dipped their branches and quivered in quiet response to the spoken words. Some had faces, some did not. Some had the suggestion of features but only if the starlight hit them just right. *I'll admit, I don't know much about dryads.* Until a couple of months ago, Daphne was the only one I'd met. But looking around at the crowd of eerily sentient saplings, I realized I knew less than I thought.

"I will speak and you will answer only when bidden." The cypress gave me another jab to punctuate her instruction. It was too close to my womb and its precious cargo. Plus, she had no authority over me. I could snap her head right off her body and shove it in the cedar's fiery mouth. I could rip the clingy arms off those oaks and beat the unpleasant little pine into literal pulp. But I wouldn't. It could take weeks to search the swamp for the witch, and something told me there was no removing the dryads from the equation.

I gritted my teeth and nodded.

Slowly, the spear left my side. The roots of the majestic cypress tightened into legs. Branches merged into long, graceful arms. The cypress straightened her back and smoothed her leaves into long flowing green hair. Her face shortened to a length and size that fit her new proportions nicely. I marveled at the new symmetry of her pale features. In fact, her humanoid countenance was so convincing, I almost believed the tree version of her to be the ruse. But one look at the blasted slits of her eyes and I knew this being had never been anything else but a swamp spirit. A broken, burned creature of the wood.

She stooped and cupped a bit of lake water into her hands then stepped onto the mushy ground of the hammock Her feet sunk as deeply as an elephant's as she lovingly poured the water into the cedar's mouth. Steam hissed. The deep glow buried inside the cedar dimmed a little. Something wordless passed through the air between them.

"Where is my mate?" She turned the charred crevices of her eyes to me. Her voice shook with the violin strings of unshed tears.

"Um, what?"

"We tracked you from the parking lot of the human Welcome Center. You travel alone. You promised that he would be returned."

"The willow isn't here?"

Unchained emotions raced across her face. Delicate fingers lengthened into sharp wooden darts.

I held my hands out as half shield and half surrender. I didn't want a fight.

"No." She threw the word at me.

The ground shook with angry roots.

This endeavor had just gotten a whole lot more complicated.

"He has performed his duty. He should have been returned to you weeks ago." Did the dryads acknowledge weeks as a unit of time? *He has performed his duty*—I sounded as callous as the Council.

"The moon has swelled and died and swelled again and still he is not among us." Her words dripped venom. "You have harmed him."

"No, no. We haven't har—"

Oh, Lesser Gods.

The Underhill.

The willow should have been released and transported home long before now. Had the Underhill taken out its frustration on the tree? Had the lovesick underground mountain crushed Daphne's temporary lover into a thousand wooden splinters. I pictured a bonfire of dryad parts piled at the bottom of the Passage of Time, and stacked on the top of the kindling—the poor tree's petrified cock—a warning to all who dared touch Dr. Daphne Willowine.

This was bad.

This was really bad.

Could the missing dryad have something to do with why the Underhill had closed?

"Well, this segways nicely into why I'm here." I smiled too widely. "Something has gone wrong inside our home. Are you familiar with the underhills?"

"We know of the Faerie Lands." The cedar's words sizzled past the quickly evaporating lake water. By this point, everyone knew at least something about the pocket universes folded into the planet's crust. Some viewed underhills as places of banishment for a variety of creatures Adam's lord no longer wanted. Others saw the Faerie Lands as strongholds, lands in which to thrive away from the polluting presence of man.

"Okay, good. Well—" I'd travelled a long way to get to that moment, but now that I was there, I had no idea what to say. "As I said, it seems—" The trees leaned in. "—that something has happened inside the Maryland Underhill."

The dryads watched me from the unblinking crags of their bark.

"The conduits between this world and ours have sealed." A small branch crashed down from the canopy and clunked a small tree in its partially formed head. No reaction registered on its empty face. I continued. "If your willow—"

"Greenstalker," the cypress snapped. "His name is Greenstalker."

I gave a slow nod in the sweltering starlight.

"If Greenstalker is still in the pocket universe, he's trapped with everyone else."

Trees shivered. Leaves fell like giant, poorly-timed confetti.

"You must open a Way."

"I'd love to, but—"

"No." Her long fingers sharpened to needles. The tips gouged the sodden earth like enormous push pins. "You will honor your promise. You will return him." The cypress shook with rage and anguish. Sometimes, I really hated my job.

"I will do everything I can to open the Way and find him."

"The words of a guileful Lilith." She paced, looking at me from every angle. "Yes, I know your kind."

"We are both children of Adam's first wife," I reminded.

"We are not as you. We do not prey upon other living things."

I wanted to argue, but as I said before, I didn't know much about dryads, so I circled back.

"As it stands now, there is no communication moving in or out of the Underhill, but I did receive one short missive. One lone directive...'bring the swamp witch.' "

The trees backed away far enough to reveal that the moon had just risen over the east side of the lake. It hung low in the sky looking very much like it had been sawed in half.

Bark cracked. Wood groaned. The smaller trees scuttled back, retreating into a thick stand of sweet gum maples on a neighboring hammock.

I waited again as the giant flora entities conversed in their wordless language. Finally, the pale tree woman turned to me.

"It is not possible to *bring* the witch anywhere."

"Why not?"

"She does not leave the swamp."

"The Council of Elders have extractors who are pretty persuasive."

"Are these extractors locked in your underhill?"

How do you humans say…touché?

"*I* can be pretty persuasive." I flicked my powerful wings and flexed my talons.

"Do yu intnd to nthrall hr wth yr sexul charms?" The knotty pine's sticky words gummed up my eardrums.

"If I must." I took a step toward the hunched creature and let the smallest piece of my eros slip free. Branches quivered. Needles danced. I let another sliver of desire lift into the night air for good measure. Bark flowed. Trunks wobbled. My particular form of enchantment worked on males and females alike. If I wanted, I could turn this swampy island into a buggy palace of love quicker than you could say sapphic circle jerk.

"Mocking a sex faerie about her source of power is a deliciously dangerous impulse."

"You stir things within us we have not felt since the swamp was new…sister." The ancient cedar's trunk rippled, bark tightened, massive curves bulged from a decidedly feminine trunk. I appreciated the acknowledgement.

"There's plenty to go around." Eros rose to the surface of my skin. I held it in check, but the energy crackled around me, filling the soupy air with possibilities. Like moths to swamp light, the younger trees returned, sucking and pulling at the mud with their strong, probing roots.

The evening turned, as evenings do, when the priorities of the flesh drown out all others. Even the cypress woman with her back rigid with rage and face wet with lake water tears softened around the edges. Her arms relaxed. Her fingers shortened.

"This solves nothing," she whispered as her hands roamed her sleek, hard form.

She was right, but I needed a guide to lead me to the Swamp Witch. If I needed to fuck my way to that goal then so be it.

Carefully, I reached a hand toward her striated waist. Delicate blotches of driftwood gray created a transition from her pale legs to her ash brown torso. My fingers brushed the speckled wood and met warmth, tender bark, and a surprising pliability. The sensation reminded me of the times I'd bumped into Daphne in the lab. The startling softness of my friend's skin always astonished me.

Daphne. My thoughts formed an arrow pointing north toward the Underhill and all the souls trapped inside. Particularly...Hamus.

Night Mother. Where had that thought come from?

Fire. Fear. Iridescent scales flashing with heat.

Lilith.

I'd barely had a moment to reel in my accidental, split-second, microscopic pondering when I heard it. The voice came from nowhere and everywhere.

"Hamus?" I swayed under the enormity of his call. The sudden pulling inside me threatened to turn me inside out. I lost control of my eros. It flooded the hammock. The forest. It soaked into the lake.

As if he had never left, as if he were a parasite dug deep into my brain, Hamus looked at me from the inside of my head. His presence filled me, pouring into me like steaming lake water in my mouth. Just like it had that first time, a month ago, in the Everglades when I'd teetered on the edge of death.

"H—how?" The audacious question bloomed in the space we now shared. Was Hamus's power really that strong? He was an elder. A ruler of his realm. A progenitor of many lines of fae. Heat rose in that new place—the place that held my secret cravings. The luscious location inside me that yearned for the attention of a strong, authoritative man. A man in charge. A man who could praise me or punish me. A man who saw me as the good girl I wanted to be...and the bad girl who needed control, who needed lessons, who need a firm hand.

Passion uncoiled at my core. Fire bloomed inside Hamus's eyes. He lifted his hand. His sturdy, dominant hand. It felt so close, as if it could reach through the dimensions and—

Oh, Lesser Gods.

I opened my eyes.

The hammock laid out before me in writhing ruins.

I'd broken the swamp.

8

NIGHT HERON

73% Black-crowned Night Heron

27% Tricolored Heron

I gasped in the thick night air as fireflies twinkled above the shuddering mass of twining roots and clutching hands. Trunks split into hungry legs. Tongues searched. Fingers found. Moans of heart-quaking pleasure rolled over the downed forest. The knot of dryads slipped in and out of humanoid form as the ground took on a throbbing heartbeat of ecstasy. The lake grew gasping mouths as creatures of sinew and scales flashed just beneath its surface.

A squirming crater of rapture spread out across the bramble-covered swells and drowning ditches transforming the northern bank of the lake into a bowl of delirium. And I stood at its center laving at the rhapsodies of sensation. Drinking the life force of every living thing. Relishing the fleshy greed, the violent release. I beat my wings until I hovered over the choking, spasming, feasting throng, a dark star of purpose. A ravaging angel.

I could have lived in that moment forever. I could have built a temple of devasting euphoria on that sinking mire. Not a hermit's nest of boulders on a secluded mountain top, but a palace of razor sweet agony, an opulent den of sensual delights. I could be what the Night Mother had intended me to be...an all-consuming force of carnal delight and destruction.

No sooner had I tried the crown on for size than I was knocked from my sovereign seat.

A pale blue ball of wobbling light struck me in the chest. I went down in a blinding tangle of feathers and mud. Before I could get my feet under me, another ball streaked across my right wing, singing the soft down at the bend of my elbow.

Hollow flames danced along my arms and legs eating at my tank top and burning holes in my best shorts. The foulness of rotting eggs filled my mouth and nose. I squeezed my eyes shut and leapt for the lake. Another blast of heat crashed into my back driving me into the waiting water.

A whirling surge of silky slick bodies wrapped around me. Hands gripped. Lips fastened. Teeth sawed. I sank to the silty bottom of the shallow lake as manic mouths threatened to suck the very marrow from my bones, but the fire was doused. One problem at a time.

I tucked my wings close and did my best to anchor myself to the snarl of submerged branches and forest detritus. Another blob of warping fire streaked over the surface of the lake. I held my breath until the light died, leaving me in the grip of the wriggling shadows and suckling mouths. Fins ruffled. Ridges rippled. Torsos undulated in a bumping, winding dance along my skin.

I could hold my breath a long time, but not forever. It was time to assess my situation. I'd come to the swamp under the cover of dark to find the dryads and secure their help in finding the Swamp Witch, a personage I'd never met, and convince said personage to travel with me to Baltimore and save a pocket universe of lying, scheming fae.

So far, I thought I was doing swimmingly.

Pun intended.

The reality of my situation was that I couldn't fly again until my feathers were dry, and I really needed to breathe. I'd just made up my mind to breach the surface and storm what constituted the beach, when a shadow blotted out the moonlight above me. The tilting, rolling surface of the sediment-clouded water blurred the long-legged figure wading toward me. Moonlight silhouetted the towering form as it hunched over the water's surface. It had navigated the maze of waterlogged wood with ease and now hovered still as death, peering at me. Long, spindly fingers reached through the turbulence of cold-blooded bodies coiling around me. Its face drew close. Closer. Eyes shone alligator bright beneath a folded brow of twigs and worms and centipede legs. Bone-bleached antlers reached from the dark muddle of snakes and thorny brambles crowning its head. Its midnight skin whispered with pale blue flames.

I bunched my legs—talons up—and prepared to rip my way out of this encounter, but even as I lunged, its dredging fingers found my arms and yanked me skyward.

"Leave this place." The water turned its words into deep, rolling things. With a neck-breaking lurch, I broke the surface, gasping for breath. "Leave now." A cotton soft voice whispered in my ear. I turned my aching neck so that I could face this new horror.

Soft brown eyes met my gaze with too much white showing around them. Petunia pink lips tensed. Chocolate cheeks glittered with water or maybe tears. The girl relaxed her grip on my arms and I kicked away. She held so still in the water, if it weren't for her pale nightgown floating and dragging in the dark water, I would have sworn she was a ghost, a mirage, a frozen after-image trapped inside my mind's eye. Where had the monster gone?

The human girl of maybe ten years lifted one dripping finger to her lips.

"Go quiet, or they'll hear." Her other hand lifted from the water and another small finger pointed west.

"Are—are you the Swamp Witch?"

"Shh!" A fine tremor shook her down to the curly ends of her bird's nest hair. The whites of her eyes glowed with fear.

"I do not fear the trees."

"Go now, or you'll lead them right to us." Her gaze slid to the lake and the trees on the east side of the swamp. Something told me the little girl wasn't talking about the dryads.

A chill settled over me. Reluctantly, I turned from her and scanned the far side of the water with my owlish vision. Nothing moved in the shadows but distant night herons and the occasional leaping fish.

When I turned back to the little human, she'd come so close that barely a breath would fit between us. I stumbled back.

"Please listen—" I held my hands out as she slowly advanced on me. "I'm here to help the trees. I know where their missing dryad is. He's locked inside my underhill." I tripped over my words as I searched her wide eyes for any sense of recognition. "I—I need help."

I fell over a jutting log and went under. Alligator eyes peered down at me from the thick night air. Bone white antlers loomed. When I emerged, the little girl had stopped her forward movement. I wiped my wet eyes with the back of my even wetter hand. The water. The girl had some kind of glamour and the lake water was interfering with it. I knew I would regret my next words. "I need the Swamp Witch." My heart thundered in my chest. My breath wheezed from my lungs. I'd faced nameless horrors, forgotten gods, demonic multitudes, and had never had such a sense of creeping dread. This entity was outside my sphere of understanding. If she wasn't the Swamp Witch, then she was an unaccompanied human minor standing in a lake in the middle of a treacherous swamp. At night. That scared me. A lot.

Her small head tilted. Her soft brown eyes blinked. I waited as a strange sense of presence flowed into her face. I couldn't put my finger on exactly what had been missing before, but whatever it was, it had returned to her like a bird at the roosting hour.

"Who are you?" Her small voice shrank even further.

"I am Lilith," I offered calmly. No sudden moves. "I've come on behalf of Greenstalker."

"You are the one who took him." Something pale and blue lit in her eyes.

"Yesss, but I'm here now to help get him back."

The fire spread from her eyes to her face. It raced over the cloud of her hair and leapt to her thin arms. The tiny lost human cupped her hands and shaped the flames into a wobbly ball.

"Wait, please. We need your help. Greenstalker and many others are trapped underground. The last instruction I received was to find you and bring you to the Underhill."

She shook her head from side to side with the violence of a human child facing down the broccoli on her dinner plate.

"I do not leave the swamp."

Bring the Swamp Witch. Hurry. I recalled the words burned into Daniel's floor. Could I force this creature? Something wild and tucked into the deepest part of my hindbrain said no. Reason with her.

"It's the only way to bring Greenstalker back."

The prepubescent child looked up at me with shock and mistrust, then turned and picked her way smoothly to shore.

"I can take you there and bring you right back. Please consider—"

"I *cannot* leave the swamp." She shout-whispered through gritted teeth. The witch scoured the eastern shore of the lake squinting at every glint of moonlight, every splash of water. "If I leave, the slavers will find me." The small girl's eyes swam with ghosts. "They will take me back to the plantation. The swamp can't protect me there." She blinked the spirits away and pulled herself up onto the soggy ground.

"Wait. Did you say slavers?" I gaped, then shot another look around the lake. "There are no more slavers."

Right?

The haunted child didn't acknowledge my words. Had she even heard me?

I blundered through the underwater obstacle course and joined her on the writhing hammock. Roots thrashed. Bodies jerked. I knew the human rules about children and sex so I put my body between her and the carnal display.

The gesture seemed unnecessary as the young girl's gaze was far away. Her arms lifted as her unfocused eyes floated in her cherub face. Pale blue light danced along her skin. Behind me the marshy island came alive with the sounds of wood cracking and mud sucking. I turned to see the swampy woods reviving itself. Trees sat up and got to their feet. Roots sank back into their murky hiding places. Branches reached for cleansing the moonlight. The haze of desire lifted from the dryads like wandering fog. But things were left in its place. Yearnings long forgotten bloomed on craggy faces. Connections deepened in the heartwood. And something else. Something beyond the bonds of love. I read it in their glances. The way their hands hung empty at their sides. Something was missing. A necessity.

I turned back to the young girl who no longer looked so young. She wore a heaviness. A burden.

"You have violated them." She regarded me from beneath that unknowable weight. "You have also reminded them of what they have lost...and what is to come."

I looked to the dryads. To the trees both young and old. To the swamp, a vestige of some prehistoric ocean. An abiding footprint of the Father Who Turned Away. And I knew. I knew what they'd lost. I knew what hung in the balance.

"Survival."

The Swamp Witch took a spot next to me and examined the grove of living wood. Were the dryads a whimsy? A bit of wild magic lost in the woods? Or were they an ordained creation as worthy of life as the rest of Lilith's children? Daphne was worthy. I had to believe that Greenstalker and his folk had just as much right to walk this world.

"Will you leave them like this to ponder their slow demise?"

I gave the witch a confused glance. Was she saying what I thought she was saying?

"You can give them what they need most." Her eyes had grown older. Tired. "You can give them a chance at new life."

It turned out that she was, in fact, saying what I thought she was saying. I could call the seed of any male. I'd been summoned as a fallback plan for many unsuccessful breeding attempts at the lab. But we'd already taken the dryads' only male.

"Until Greenstalker is returned, I'm not sure there is anything I can do."

The girl nodded. Moonlight gathered in the sap at the corner of every dryad's eyes.

"Greenstalker is our only breeding male." Her thin fingers reached through the buzzing, clicking, chirping night. A tongue of flame almost too dim to distinguish from the fireflies danced then dove from her fingertip into the darkness and disappeared. Moments later something shoved from the shadows, crawled through mud, shimmied past trunks.

A narrow tree with a muscular trunk but reed thin roots and fidgeting arms came to the witch's call. A starlight blue flame flickered along the dryad's smooth face. Caressing its cheek, reflecting in its wide, nervous eyes. An oak from the look of its leaves and long, bark-covered legs.

The flame gave the oak tree one last lingering lick then leapt back to the witch's tiny hand. It disappeared into her palm taking its light with it.

"This is Mistrunner."

The wary oak tensed at the mention of his name. Maybe the dryads didn't speak their names in human languages often. Maybe this was its very first time hearing the collection of sounds that identified it to creatures other than trees.

"Mistrunner, son of Dusktreader, you have reached the age of reason. Do you seek a place among your sisters?" The witch's words seemed too old, too formal for her small voice. But I had only focused on one word—*son*.

The male dryad looked from elder to elder, then realized he was being asked to speak. He cleared his timber throat.

"I do." Two quick words, rough and deeply male.

I studied him. His tense, woody muscles, shy mouth, worried eyes, clenching fists. Was this the saving grace of the Great Dismal Dryads? Or was this a tree about to bolt and never be heard from again?

One way to find out.

I shook the water from my dripping wings and slinked over to him. One of Mistrunner's thin roots slid behind him, but the rest held their ground. I came to a stop only inches from his slender trunk. Long muscles, square shoulders, strong branches. The tree looked down at me with fascinated eyes. But patches of the dryad were unfinished. Important zones seemed undeveloped. Namely the space between his legs. Wood bulged in the right place, but the swell was smooth and lacking the equipment needed for proper insemination. Was this how all dryads started regardless of physical gender? Or just males?

Lucky for Mistrunner, I liked a challenge.

9

LEMMING

100% Southern Bog Lemming

*O*kay, humans. If you don't want to hear how the naughty succubus robbed the sweet, tender tree of his virginity, then cover your ears. Whistle your favorite tune. Or go get a snack.

For everyone else, I'll share a thought with you that I've put a bit of research into. It's my belief that a person's first sexual encounter sets the tone not just for how they'll view fucking from there on out, but also how they'll view themselves as lovers. Was the experience thrust on them? Were their desires denied? Were they forced into the wrong role? Missteps like this could ruin sex for a beginner for years.

If ever you find yourself in the role of deflowerer, remember that there is more at stake than just one knocking of boots. Consider it your honor to guide someone onto a path of healthy, kinky, orgasmic smashing. Trust me, they'll spend a lifetime looking back on their experience with you and smiling.

And maybe touching themselves.

I had to give Mistrunner credit for not flinching. He'd likely never been handled by a humanoid before and his first encounter was with, of all things, a succubus. With luck like that, he really should play some lottery numbers.

I started by gently smoothing my hands down his mossy back. The sparse patches of fuzzy green indicated that he'd stood facing south a long time. I wondered about the lives of vegetative beings. What was it like to awaken and grow through the long, sweltering months of summer and silently dream through the icy rain and winter wind. As a dryad, he could have changed his orientation. What had been so compelling to the south that he'd chosen to face it every day through the blinding sunlight? The lake was south. Was there something in its waters that called to him?

I touched his leaves. A shiver ran through him. I cupped his chin. His jaw tightened. Anxiety over the unknown swam in his amber eyes like shadowy fish. He was ready, but fearful. He'd just watched from the safety of the nearby sweet gum grove as my power flattened his people like grass. He had a right to be concerned.

"What are you waiting for?" The witch's wispy voice frosted over. I turned to see if the antlered, alligator-eyed version of the little girl had returned. It hadn't. If anything, the witch looked to have aged backward a human year or two.

"I'm waiting for a deal to be struck."

"No one makes deals with faeries." I knew what she meant was—no one with *sense in their skulls* made deals with the fae.

"A simple trade." I offered. "I will bring this fine young specimen into breeding condition if you travel to the Maryland Underhill with me and help us...fix it." I could have finished that sentence in a lot of ways, but I needed to keep the verbiage general. Chaos dwelled inside this creature, but I sensed so much more. There was no telling how she might interpret the barter.

"I will not travel with you."

"Then, travel on your own. Meet me at the portal inside the Flora and Fauna Laboratory at Hans Jodkins University in Baltimore tomorrow morning."

Her soft gaze slid to the side as she pondered. After a moment, those innocent eyes found mine again.

"Agreed."

Thank the Night Mother.

"Do you require directions?"

The innocence drained from her eyes.

"Fine. The trade is struck."

My part of the deal was easy. I had no idea how this little creature would handle a shuttered pocket universe with a seismic temper, but that wasn't my problem.

I turned to the dryad and tried to keep the carnivore out of my smile. I folded my wings against my back and replaced my human glamour.

"Do you prefer this?"

Beads of sweat fought through his thin bark. He shook his head.

I took a step toward him and adjusted my rainbows. I wasn't a master at sensory magic, but beguiling was a talent of mine. A few alterations on-the-fly and my skin cooled to a shimmering green. My thighs fused into a skirt of sparkling scales. My feet spread into a curling mermaid tail.

The tree's buried heart thumped so hard I feared his wood might crack. His gaze jerked toward the water. The lake. To the south.

Trees quaked around us. A few of the smaller pines with mouths gasped.

Had I stumbled into taboo territory? Had I revealed a secret?

The dryad shook his head again, but this time he put some energy into it.

I stepped close and gave him an apologetic glance. I smoothed my rainbows into craggy bark. Twisted my hair into spring soft branches.

"There's no need to be nervous," I whispered into his ear. "I imagine you've withstood storms, brushfires, gnawing insects. This is so much easier." I let the smallest pulse of eros soak into his trunk. Charcoal pupils yawned wide. Roots swelled. The night filled with the brushing of leaves as the smaller trees retreated once more to the neighboring island. I peered behind me, but the witch was gone. Only the largest and oldest trees remained.

Fine by me.

I trailed a finger down the dryad's heaving chest and thought of the other male, the one we'd taken. Greenstalker. He'd been conflicted too. When I'd walked him into the Copulation Room back at the Underhill's lab, he'd refused to cooperate. Daphne had been there too, looking ravishing in her lab coat and nothing else. I remembered the way her greenish-blonde hair fell in a long, shiny curtain around her narrow shoulders. The way it clung like tiny waterfalls to her tight, pink nipples as she'd slowly removed her lab lanyard and coat. Something had passed between them in that cramped, clinical space. They'd been strangers. But they'd swayed in the same ropey way, emitted the same meadow green fragrance, hid their thoughts behind the same screen of long silky hair. They were both willows. Regardless of where their affections lay, wood spoke to wood as flesh speaks to flesh.

I looked around at the gathering of lusty-eyed trees. Two dryads held the same leaf patterns as Mistrunner. The twins. Their craggy eyes fixed on the young male like a falcon's. Their hands clutched. Their arms tightened. They waited in a squirming knot as my finger trailed lower. I stopped just above the tantalizing mound between his barky legs. If Mistrunner was anything like Greenstalker, something delicious waited in that sleeping wood. I would find the best way to coax it out.

I know what you're thinking—why not just drown him in eros and force his wood to rise. Well, dear humans, when it comes to the first intimacy—there are no do-overs. You get one chance to make the core memory shine. So, sit down, shush, and let me do my thing.

Beyond the buzzing of insects, past the whooping of owls and twanging of frogs, there are quieter things. Like the wetting of lips, the heaving of breaths, the flutter of uncertain hearts. I listened for those gentle sounds. Trapped them in my hands. Rolled them in my mouth, then mimicked them. Quietly, at first. Then, louder, stronger, with a delicate urgency that coaxed my lover's body to react in kind. He breathed, I breathed. He quivered, I quivered. Slowly, we began the dance of alignment, the sweet surrender to synchronicity.

Our fingertips met as if touching a mirror. A warm, safe sameness that promised to reflect all that we had ever craved. All that we'd needed but couldn't ask for.

Mistrunner's muscles relaxed.

Inside the safety of our tandem heartbeats there was room for more. A caress. A cautious stroke. Nothing intrusive. Just a series of gentle invitations. Once accepted, those enticements gave way to feathery quests, quick rummaging explorations.

Mistrunner sighed.

I answered that sweet music with a soft, pleading breath. A sound he seemed to want more of. His hands closed on my breasts, springing flesh, tickling tips, soft treasures that called forth a thready moan from my throat. His heartbeat sprinted like a racer at the sound of a starting pistol.

There it was—the first of my lover's traits. He was a pleaser.

I indulged him. Guided him to the parts of me with the greatest reward. A few more hungry grips and his hand found its way past my shorts and between my legs to the river of desire waiting to drench his fingers. I gasped as he delved into my special anatomy. He eagerly plundered my turgid venereae layers seeking that bright bulge. That small mound of fiery delight. I panted as he worshipped it like a priceless gem. Coaxed it like a downy, spring hatchling. He foraged for every soft sound he could elicit from me. I covered his hand with mine and showed him how to work me. How to make me buck. I held back the dam of eros that threatened to break free with every graze of his fingertips. He clutched me close as he experimented with different pressures, varying speeds. I danced against him, filling his ear with a mindless begging. I slid my hand slowly, carefully between his legs over the heated mound of straining wood.

His tongue found my mouth, thick yet supple. I opened for him. Let him fill me. His fingers sank past my petals into the drowning tunnel at my core.

I let a desperate lick of eros escape. It perfumed the air, sinking through wood and earth. Our little audience moaned in response.

My leafy lover removed his hand, withdrew his tongue, and knelt on the spongy ground in front of me.

"Give me more," he demanded.

There it was—the second of my lover's traits. He was dominant. A fresh forceful energy spread through the hammock. If this encounter was for my benefit, I would have gladly spread my legs and complied like a good little submissive. But this night was not for me. It was for him...and for them.

I stepped away from my breathless young lover and reached for the pair of females sliding against each other in desperate need. They came willingly.

Mistrunner offered a tentative hand to the curvy oak on the right while I guided the lithe creature to the left to sit with me on a thicket of soft grass. A pair of fuzzy, little lemmings raced from the flattened clump as we settled. Eros leaked from my skin as I watched my pupil build a bridge of intimacy with his new partner. I caressed my new lover as we watched Mistrunner and the voluptuous oak explore each other with hungry grasps and frantic embraces. The oak bent forward and their mouths met in a devouring kiss. He filled his hands with her substantial breasts.

"Lie down," I whispered to my trembling oak. She complied with rapt delight.

"Do you want to make them really happy?" I ran a hand down Mistrunner's back. He turned an entranced face to me.

"Yes," he answered enthusiastically.

My lips spread into the toothy grin of a predator knee deep in entrails. This was my domain. The kingdom of rapture.

I eased the shuddering oak onto her back and slid my hands to her thighs. With a delicious slowness, I eased her legs apart. Leaves floated down on us as the trees around us trembled and quaked.

Mistrunner collected the other oak in his arms and laid her on the ground next to her bonded mate. I knelt between my new lover's legs. I breathed her breaths. I fluttered with her shivers. I introduced my lips to her thighs. I acquainted my tongue with her pulpy moisture. Drawing ever closer to that sweet division of flesh. To the welcoming folds of her inner self. She spread for my hot breath. She laid herself bare for the sweet agony of my touch.

With a precision built into my Carnem nature, my tongue lit the match of her aching flesh. She cried out, igniting the flame inside Mistrunner to learn this arcane talent. He took equal care in exposing his lover, in teasing her to just the right point. He watched as I delved into the delicate places. Then, tasted those places for himself. He observed as I measured my lover's responses and altered my tricks. He mimicked my strategies as I both gave my lover what she wanted and withheld it at the same time. From the whimpers of his lover, I could tell he was a fast-learner.

Together, we worshipped at the altar of womanhood. We lapped every drop of their sweet, heady sap. We teased them to the pinnacle of pleasure. We fed on their surrender. We took the twins on the ride of their lives. And when they could endure no more, we let them ride our flicking tongues to thundering release.

Dangerous levels of eros rose inside me. If it had been perilous for me to orgasm with the Children of the First Wife before, now that I was super-charged with mana, I could only find satisfaction with the strongest of my kind. These gentle trees were not they. I needed to accomplish my goal and get back into the Underhill where I belonged.

Hurry. A voice echoed in my head from far away.

Mistrunner leaned back on his heels reveling in his new power. Our small audience had enjoyed the show. They franticly worked their bodies. Moaning with delight.

"Now is your time to become all that you can be." I took his hand. We stood in the circle of female eruptions. The swampy air ignited with ecstasy. One by one the dryads rode their own waves to dizzy release. And I fed.

"Please." His face took on a pained expression.

I pressed my hands over the cracking wood between his legs and funneled a healthy dose of eros through my palms. Wood shattered; splinters launched in every direction. My hands blew back as Mistrunner's new anatomy crashed free. I joined the collective gasp as his translucent member steamed in the moonlight. The stony column hung from his body like a missile bulging from its silo.

Lesser Gods. The rumors were true. Male dryads really did have the best wood.

"Now is the time—when they are relaxed and well lubricated." I pointed at the spent women languishing on the hammock's soggy bed. "Take them," I whispered to the dominant male newly awakened at the heart of the swamp.

I watched with gnawing desire as the strong, young male dragged his lover to her feet, bent her over and fucked her until she spasmed around his giant pillar. With a last shuddering thrust he spurted his seed until it overflowed and ran down her legs. Joyous cries drowned out the owls and frogs.

A few deep breaths later, he pulled his other lover to her feet, positioned her until her ass pointed to the sky. Then, he rubbed the glassy head of his torpedo against her eager opening and, like the fast-learner he was, teased her with it. He dragged it along her sensitive peak, coated it in her slippery juices, then pushed just the head in. He shook with the effort, but managed to draw it out.

"No," she cried. "Give it to me," she begged in vocal words, but I sensed she'd also spoken in the silent language of trees as well. His every muscle tensed with the need to explode again. Slowly, he buried his swollen cock into her tight tunnel until he reached the end of her. "Yes," she cried. Her leg muscles danced. Her back bowed. It was all he could take. Mistrunner gripped her hips and rammed her over and over. Spanking her with his body. Stretching her. Filling her. Making her his. She gave her voice to the night as she convulsed on his greedy cock. He buried himself deep and joined the chorus of release. He held her on his shaft as he spurted inside her. Wailing with each gush of seed. Thick fluid drooled down both their legs.

The deed was done. My part of the bargain was fulfilled.

The oaks collapsed in a heap of quivering muscles and satisfaction. The cedar, the pine, and the woeful cypress found my gaze in the moonlight.

"Thank you," the cedar choked. Tears steamed down her majestic, heated face. "Now, go get our brother."

I nodded. My eyes darted to the pale tree, but she was already turning away, sinking back into the warm, shallow waters of

Lake Drummond. The witch was nowhere to be found. I could only hope that she would make good on her side of the trade. It was in her best interest to do so. Breaking a promise to a fae could get messy.

I turned north, away from the lake and the woman I'd wronged. I spread my mostly dry wings and took to the air. I had a few pixies trapped in the glove compartment of Daniel's Jeep. I'd need the extra kilo calories not just for the drive home, but for what would come next.

Like any good fae, I was compelled to do the bidding of the Council. The pressing drive to open a conduit into the Underhill clawed at me. Probably increased by my pregnancy and the need to be within the boundaries of the Faerie Lands for my children's births. *That's all this urgency is, Lilith. It has nothing to do with that worthless draco demon.*

I landed near the parking lot, grabbed the keys to Daniel's Jeep off the tire, and tore out of there. I prayed to the Night Mother to turn all the stoplights from here to Baltimore green.

I'm coming.

10

SWAMP WITCH

9% Human

91% Unknown Plantae-Animalia Fusion

I stood in the women's restroom in Building D of the Flora and Fauna Lab and stared at the wall. Hans Jodkins University had other portals to the Underhill, but they were quite public. The Swamp Witch, if she showed up, would not appreciate an audience. That is why I specified the gateway here in the Flora and Fauna lab. I was one of the only fae to use this opening. It was as private as we were going to get.

I pulled at the waist band of my pencil skirt. Had I eaten too many pixies? Or were my extra occupants starting to need more room? I turned and looked myself over in the mirror. Despite a half a night of pacing the laboratory halls with my vagabond bag of meager possessions in tow, my human hair still hung in shiny brown waves over my shoulders. My eyes still looked rested, though I was anything but. I'd added a little extra gloss to my glamoured lips and a petal pink eyeshadow to match my summer blossom blush.

Despite the addition of a few black streaks and a bit of lavender around the edges of my face, I was the woman Daniel had fallen in love with once again. The thought of him brought the quiet ache in my chest to the forefront of my mind until it was all I could feel.

Falling for a human—*stab*.

Revealing myself to said human and still being accepted—*stab, stab*.

Fucking said human without killing him—*stab, stab, stab*.

He and I still needed to have a conversation about that fossil he wore around his neck. Fae magic was not tamable by human means. And all of it was dangerous. But he'd not been at the apartment when I'd arrived last night. So, I'd taken a shower, put on fresh clothes, packed my few possessions, and left the keys in the bowl by the door.

I wondered if he'd ever speak to me again. *Why did I even want him to?* I was a knocked-up night monster under an ancient curse that would take my life in a matter of months. This was not the time to agonize over some human crush.

"Lilith, you're an idiot," I whispered to the woman in the mirror.

"I agree." A deep, bass voice vibrated through the walls of the women's bathroom.

"Domov?" I whirled around as my hairy, little friend materialized from the wall. I stared with my mouth agape at the three-foot homunculus. The tiny threshold fae was the first denizen of the Underhill I had laid eyes on since I'd left for my

Florida vacation. "What are you doing here? Is the Underhill open again?"

"My business is my own and no, the Underhill is definitely still closed."

"But—" I pointed toward the wall from which he'd just stepped, but I realized I'd not seen the rock chewing circle of interdimensional egress. Domov was a member of the Apercula Family, Genus Intervallum. He could open a door through almost anything. He was a creature of the between places. If he wanted to hover in the walls of the women's restroom with the plumbing and electrical wires like a proper perv, who was I to judge?

"I am keeping an eye on the less travelled paths."

And the ladies with their underpants around their ankles, I thought to add, but it was hard to judge what a fae-in-thrall would find amusing. Domov was one of the oldest terrestrial fae, but his nature had been warped, like so many of the Night Mother's first children, by forces I didn't fully understand. And as a fae-in-thrall, Domov the Clean was in a constant state of servitude to other fae. He needed all the entertainment he could get.

As our elder, we should be serving him, but that was not his lot in life. In fact, you might remember my not so little mistake some weeks ago when I'd accidentally spoken his full name out loud. It was the rudest of summonings. I still hadn't forgiven myself.

From the tone of his voice, he hadn't forgiven me either.

"Domov—" I began, but an overt apology would be distasteful as well. There were so many rules with the Old World fae. Can't a girl just say *sorry*?

He gave me a look weighed down by not just my fresh slight but by centuries of wrongs. How could the Father Who Turned Away have allowed such a thing as genetic slavery?

"Do not speak of it, child." His gaze dropped to the floor.

It was big of him to let me off the hook so easily. I'd embarrassed my friend. I cared about that wee man. In the Underhill, true affection was hard to find. I think neither one of us wanted to throw a friendship away over something less than blood-letting.

"It's good to see you," I held the tears in check.

"It is good to be seen."

"I received a message on my way home from Florida. The Council warned me to stay away, but they didn't offer a reason. By the time I made it to the East Gate portal, it had closed. They'd all closed. I assume everyone from the Genetic Recombination Center is trapped inside because no one is returning my calls." I'd tried reaching Hennig Dreadmare's and Gillian Hobglen's phones in the separate Morphology Research Library, but no luck. Of course, I'd tried Daphne's number over and over, but no one was answering.

"There has been no further communication from inside this Underhill. The Ways between the other underhills and this one were sealed as well." He clarified. "I and my brethren had nothing to do with it."

I leaned against the bathroom wall which put my back closer to the bend of electricity through the rat's nest of hidden conduits pulsing in every wall of the human complex. All the machines, all the tempered metal thrummed in my head. Building D was the laboratory facility the fae shared with humans. It had been altered to help us tolerate working side by side with them and their equipment, but some areas had been missed.

"And there is still no opening them from this dimension?"

He shook his head and took a seat on the floor. I slid down the wall and joined him. I slipped my heels off and set them next to me.

"Domov, I received a message from inside…after the closure."

He gave me a startled look.

"The mountain has locked down all forms of correspondence."

"Not all." I folded my legs to the side and turned to him. "Hamus found a way to slip me an instruction using his element of fire." I pulled the burled wood cellphone from my pocket and opened the photo I'd taken of the missive burned into Daniel's floor.

"That's impossible."

I looked from him to the frequency dampened device, to him again.

"I saw it with my own eyes." Did he mean it was impossible to find the witch? "I found her in the Dismal Swamp. I don't know what she can do for us, but I'm waiting for her now." I'd already realized my mistake in rushing into the agreement with the girl. I hadn't been as specific as I could have been about time and place.

"It would be impossible for Hamus to locate you in the human dimension unless—" He regarded me with eyes so old they seemed like prototypes, pupils in an obsolete shape, irises in a discontinued color.

"Unless what?"

"Unless you were bonded."

"Ha." The sound came out of me like a bullet. I inhaled to fire off another guffaw, but Domov wasn't laughing. He stared at me with his antique eyes. Seeing more than I could.

A shiver travelled down my body.

"Wait, what?" My human phrasing held a command so I re-worded. "What do you mean 'bonded'? Like, *bonded* bonded?" My extremities went cold.

Domov opened his mouth to answer, but I cut him off.

"No, no. Hamus is a council member. He is King of the Draco Demons. He's—he's really powerful. I—I've felt his energy. If anyone could get a message out, surely, it would be him."

"He is a great and powerful king. He is a suitable mate."

No, I wasn't singing that sadistic demon's praises. Why was Domov? I was just trying to make a point, but that point would have to wait because a small, unaccompanied child had entered the bathroom.

"My apologies." Domov bowed and scuttled toward the door.

"Domov." I stood and stepped in front of him to keep him from leaving. The movement put my back to the nervous girl in the homemade dress and muddy shoes. Every hair on my neck stood up. "This is the Swamp Witch." I pointed to my cellphone and the photograph of Hamus's message. "She's here to help.

11

APPALACHIAN TIGER SWALLOWTAIL BUTTERFLY

53% Canadian Tiger Swallowtail

47% Eastern Tiger Swallowtail

Without the benefit of the lake's water, could Domov see the witch's true form? I couldn't see it with my naked eye, but I could feel it scuttling over my skin like stray centipedes. Those lantern eyes, alligator orange. Sticks and snakes and squirming things wreathing her head like a swampy crown. And the antlers—wide and tall with too many points to count. It was all there in the bathroom with us, hovering behind a tightly wrapped glamour or something very like a glamour.

Domov backed away from the eerie little girl with her cloud of kinky curls separated now into two fluffy pompoms on the top of her head. I gave her plenty of room too. She looked like a child who'd gotten lost on her way to church if the church was in the Colonial Era.

"Thank you for coming." I nodded. She studied me with her soft, innocent eyes, then returned the nod. Her gaze wandered to the wall. Reed thin legs carried her past the toilet stalls. Tiny feet shuffled to a stop in front of the thickly painted cinderblocks.

We waited, Domov and I, for long minutes as the witch stood like a grade school child placed to face the wall for bad behavior. Then, in a flash of movement, she raised her arm and smashed her tiny hand through the wall. I leapt out of my skin. Domov stumbled backward over his hairy feet. The witch leaned in, burying her arm to the shoulder in the jagged new mouth of broken cement. Her dress swished as she appeared to grope for something. At last, she withdrew her arm and turned to face us.

"I cannot reach." She spoke like a child who'd been stretching for a cookie jar set too high for her to access. I scrambled to assist her, but I had no idea how to help.

"Domov?" This was really his department. I squatted and dug through the bag I was now living out of and produced a small, dried sugar starfish. A donation in exchange for Domov's services. The tiny, orange creature had been dehydrated in a pose that looked as though it had just been out for a casual stroll when the sun decided to cook it in its tracks. "A souvenir from southern Florida."

His shocked gaze lurched to the offering. "H—how thoughtful." He took the star, admired it for a stunned moment then stashed it in his hair. I'd selected it specifically for him before I'd known about the Underhill closing. This situation called for a gift much grander than a simple starfish, but I don't think a desiccated dolphin would have been so cute.

He gave me a wary look then reached a hand toward the broken wall. Concrete ground against my eardrums. A choking cloud of cinder dust found my mouth and nose as a portion of the wall began to spin. A large circle of glowing friction appeared in the wall as Domov's magic chewed a hole not just in the bathroom, but in the universe as well. I waited for the pulverized swirl of opalescent light which heralded the arrival of a new dimension, but it didn't show. There was no translucent skim hinting at a world just beyond the glimmering detritus. The hot glow of crushed rock cooled and the portal yawned into darkness.

The Swamp Witch stared at Domov with a glimmer of child-like interest then turned her attention to the gaping maw. With fingers clasped behind her back, she leaned close to the dimensional gateway. After only a moment of peering into that vast darkness, she stepped away and turned back to us.

"Your mountain weeps." Her soft, helium words bumped along the ceiling as if looking for a way out.

I tried to picture the ill-tempered, underground entity feeling anything but vexation. I couldn't. I hadn't been to another un-derhill since I was a child so I had no idea what normal behavior for a pocket universe looked like. All I knew was our Locus Geographia was an impolite host. Of course, I had no idea what it felt like to have a multitude of blood-thirsty, magic-wielding parasites living inside me. Some of us it liked and some of us it really didn't. Even though there was no love lost between me and the Underhill, I'd come to view it as a grouchy, tough-love kind of parent. Definitely not a creature that could feel sorrow.

"Can you tell why?" I asked the question, but I feared I knew the answer so I changed my query. "Can you help it?"

The Swamp Witch tilted her pompom head to the side as if pondering my request, or trying to understand it at all. Did the alligator-eyed entity behind the glamour feel compelled to help anything outside of her swamp? She'd seemed sympathetic toward the dryads, custodial even. But the things that were necessary for true empathy were not evident in her wide, glamour-brown eyes.

"Our deal was that I would 'help you' fix it. Not that I would fix it myself."

Good grief. I'd been out-maneuvered by a child. A non-fae child.

With that cleared up, the Swamp Witch's arms exploded into vines the width of natural gas pipelines. Domov and I flattened ourselves to the floor. Ivy coiled through the bathroom. Ferns unfurled hungry green tongues. Moss spread over the cool tiles like an emerald carpet thick with snails and beetles. Blades of grass poked between my fingers. A cloud of long-winged Tiger Swallowtail butterflies fluttered to life over the sudden sward. Their yellow and black striped wings winked through the fog gathering over our heads. The child turned and the massive cables of vegetative flesh stretched from the Witch's diminutive body into the blackness beyond the wall.

The world shuddered or maybe it was just the building, or the campus, or—more to the point—the ground underneath it. Sounds stirred in the distance as if a shockwave travelled out from our green, toileted cocoon. Car horns blared. Things with weight thudded to the ground. It was everything the protestors had predicted. The anti-fae slogans and doomsday signs they hoisted just outside the university on an ongoing basis had just been validated. Allowing a fae colony to live within a human community was dangerous.

As if my life could get any worse. Now, our friendly neighborhood protestors would swell in number. On more than one occasion, I'd thought about accidentally letting a bit of my eros loose at the East Gate of the campus. Not enough to kill them. Just enough to really embarrass them in front of their ever-present news media.

But this time they were right.

A light flared at the center of Domov's portal, dim at first. It grew into an opal of shimmering light. The glow swirled around the Witch's arms.

"It's opening," Domov exclaimed, rushing through the greenery to help prop the passageway open. "The Underhill is fighting the intrusion. It won't stay open long."

The witch's arm twitched and a pale blue flame sparked to life at her shoulder. It danced along the colossal vine and leapt into the vertical pool of shivering light.

"Quickly, Lilith. The portal could close at any second."

Chaos bloomed like a vicious flower inside me.

"Where does it lead?"

"I can't tell."

I'd jumped into my share of ominous holes before. It was kind of my specialty.

What the heck? You only live once.

I backed up to the far wall and took a running leap.

Domov growled.

The Witch staggered.

I dove.

And then I was through.

12

EARTH WORM

100% Red Wiggler

Chaos had called to chaos, I guessed because I'd land-ed in the middle of madness. Great, floating boulders of metamorphic rock tumbled overhead like asteroids without a trajectory. Something dense struck the behemoth chunk of stone on which I knelt. The collision sent me skidding to the edge of what I could only assume had once been a piece of the Passage of Time. I caught myself on a narrow portion of chiseled stairs which now lay on its side. The giant hunk of mountain I clung to teetered in the dim, lava light. Thunder rolled through the seemingly endless space. Lightning sparked as tremendous shards of granite crashed into one another sending small shock-waves through my chest. I searched above me for a reassuring glimpse of rib cage or reticulated spine, but even my owlish sight could not pierce the shadows, the emptiness.

Devastation.

Utter ruin.

I fought for breath around the little earthquakes. I couldn't even begin to assess this new reality. Had the Underhill been attacked? A chunk of labyrinthine gardens spun past me flinging soil and raining wiggly, red worms. The gardens were on the upper level of our pocket universe. I could no longer tell what was up and what was down. The only constant was a fiery glow from somewhere beneath the asteroid field.

I peeked over the edge of my broken boulder. Long strata of gneiss zigzagged along the break of stone. Schist sparkled. Dark red garnets wept from the colossal wound.

"What happened to you?" I reached over the edge and smoothed a hand along the jagged fracture. I got no reply.

Movement far below caught my eye. Dark, winding silhouettes skittered along the deep red lines of lava.

"Survivors."

I had no way to get to them. I shouted through the din of crunching rock, but my voice was eaten by the thunder. I clutched the steps and looked around at the tilting, swaying sea of rock. Nothing moved in the way it should. Some hunks of stone rotated while others remained still. Giant slabs of broken living quarters sailed beneath me trailing the personal possessions of fae I hoped were long evacuated.

When I'd first returned from Florida, I'd assumed I'd be heading up a shelter for fae evacuees, but upon my arrival in Baltimore, I'd found no one. Had any fae made it out? Those already in the human realm had been warned to stay away. A wretched thought crawled around the edges of my mind. I could have ignored Hamus's message. I could have left my fellow Children of the First Wife to this fate and gone on with my life...with Daniel. Handsome, even-tempered, fairly well-endowed Daniel. At that moment, a few months of happiness in the human world looked better than floating in that endless wasted land alone. *Why do I listen to my chaos?* It always takes me from bad to worse. Always.

I spread out on my island of hovering stone and considered my life choices. That went nowhere fast, so I considered my options instead.

Option 1: sit here and wait for Domov and the Witch to open the portal again. Jump through it and never look back. I knew a lot about genetics; I could get a job in another lab. There might be an opening in the Department of Pathology. If all else failed, I could start my own fertility clinic. The perks would be amazing.

Option 2: Hmm. Opt-shun-two. Welp, I guessed that would involve me sitting up, crawling to the edge of my asteroid, and leaping down to the next one and the next one and so on until I reached the burning field of lava canals below. I could connect with the survivors in the lower kingdoms and find out how to fix this horrible mess.

Decisions. Decisions.

I'd almost come to one, when my little sanctuary of dripping garnets tipped and I slid into the talons of a very large dragon. I scraped and scratched at the stone but there was nothing to grip. Hot hooks grasped me so quickly I didn't even have a chance to fight back. The giant creature released my granite raft and gathered my legs into its other claws. I braced to be pulled apart, to watch my entrails dangle into the void. I'd be eaten in two tidy bites. A moment of mindless pain and then I'd meet the incinerator that was the inside of a dragon. But, for some reason that didn't happen. Instead, it aligned me with its body like a falcon does when flying a tasty pigeon back to its young.

Clutching me tightly, the shimmering beast dropped through the debris field. I held onto the contents of my stomach as we plummeted past fragments of earth so large they still leaked water from their hidden springs. The dragon dragged me through one of the frothy falls drenching my pencil skirt and silk blouse.

It turned at whiplash speed and made another pass through the waterfall. I gasped as the veil of freezing water drenched my hair. We dipped through tumbling rocks and sheets of dust in a dizzying drop toward the chasm floor. I held as still as a tasty pigeon on its last flight as veins of glowing lava spread out across a blackened ground below. Those burning rivers should have been many miles down, but they weren't anymore.

Heat swelled toward me in a suffocating blast. Down we went until the charred ground rushed to meet us in jagged blades of cooled magma. The dragon's burning talons released me onto the paper-thin razorblades. The fearsome formations crushed under my bare feet like spun sugar.

I'd never been to the Realm of Fire. One, the pressure and elements were too intense for a Carnem Order creature like me. Two, this was Hamus's territory. His Kingdom. There were better ways to die than to step foot in his domain. Luckily, I'd be eaten by the dragon before that menacing A-hole even knew I was here.

No, I'm not being nonchalant, I was done. Thoroughly done. You can't fight a dragon. That was Game Over. Now, quit interrupting.

I took my time turning to meet the primal beast's gaze. I wasn't sure I wanted to look death in the eye. I'd lived twenty-eight years in that stupid pocket universe and I'd successfully avoided every scaly fire drake in the realm. Up until that moment, I was able to convince myself that they weren't a real threat.

My opinion changed drastically when I faced the creature. Hot breath. Heaving sides. Blinding scales. Its head dipped low, perhaps wanting to play with its food a bit longer. But, instead, it just watched me. I'd heard somewhere that dragons were picky about their meals and if you peed on yourself, it might turn its nose up and select another meaty morsel.

I tried to focus on my bladder. Tried to summon even a dribble of urine, but every muscle in my body had locked up with fear. Just as I felt the smallest drop attempting to quiver down my urethra, the dragon leaned back and began to shrink. Wings curled backward, neck shortened, torso thinned. In the space of a few breaths, the horrific creature had condensed into a douche of equal proportions.

"Hamus." I spat, but my spit evaporated before it hit the frilly, black ground. I tried not to notice his chainmail skirt was missing. *Night Mother*, I really tried, but damn.

"Where is the Witch?"

"Up there." I pointed to where we'd just been.

"You left her on the other side of the portal?"

"I didn't really have much choice."

His eyes glowed. His lips hissed with steam.

"You were our only chance," he growled, shifting his weight. I knew what would come next—a beautiful view of his best parts just as his sparking hoof caught my jaw. Or maybe he'd punch me square in the chest and shatter my confused heart. I'd always managed to block his attacks in the nick of time, but one day, one of his strikes would connect with full force and I'd have a hole clear through my body.

If I hadn't loathed him before, snatching me up in dragon form earned him my undying hatred. But each time I reached for that hate it slipped from me like the slimy-finned shadows in Lake Drummond. *You just don't scare a person like that, particularly someone in my "condition."*

"Well, before you go wrecking the plan—whatever it is—my guess is she's still there. She's after one thing—Greenstalker."

The demon tilted his collection of spiraling horns in confusion.

"The dryad. She wants the male dryad," I clarified.

Hamus reached his fiery hands to his head and rubbed his spiky face as though he could scrub away a misfortune the Father Who Turned Away had laid there.

"Please tell me he's still drawing breath." I didn't know it was possible to feel chilled in a place as hot as the Fire Realm, but the frozen fingers of dread crept down my spine.

"He is...but not for long."

13

VOLCANUS LIZARD

100% Pygmy Volcanus Gecko

*T*rust me, *down is a direction you don't want to go when you're already at lava level.* My lungs struggled to make use of the thick, pressing air as Hamus led me on a very sweaty journey into the citadel of flames he called home. It looked like I wasn't the only one who'd gotten an up close and personal experience with a dragon. Refugees from every part of the Maryland Underhill crowded into the fire drakes' dens. The blackened crevices practically overflowed from the steep cliffs surrounding Hamus's fortress.

"Walk faster," he commanded as we threaded through tubes of cooled lava and crunched down fields of diamond-hard rubble.

Usually, I was pretty quick on my feet, but I was eating for four now and those glovebox pixies had worn off long ago.

"I need to eat."

"Your needs do not concern me."

I slowed my pace as my head began to spin.

"Do not show weakness in this place." He stopped and growled at me. His eyes drifted to the rocky ledges on either side of us.

"I haven't eaten. I haven't slept. I've done everything you've asked of me." I glared at the fire-eyed demon. "I need water."

He propped a foot on a tumbled cluster of rocks and grazed me with his signature look of disdain.

What? I looked down at my pitiful state. Steaming silk clung to my ribs, clutching my breasts in sloppy wrinkles. My soot-stained pencil skirt had ripped at the seams and I could only guess at the condition of my hair.

"There is water ahead." He pointed to the towering stronghold. The structure was very close, but I didn't see a way in. No bridges crossed the deep canyon from which it rose. No stairs wound around its outer walls. Why would he need such an impregnable fortress? Who would attack dragons and fire demons?

I took a moment to catch my breath and, yes, to ogle my naked companion. I hated him, but a girl could admire burnished muscles, sparkling scales, thick winding horns, and a cock like a fire hose. Pun intended.

Hamus followed my gaze to his manly masterpiece, then drew a line with his finger just above his nethers. That molten gold skirt of chainmail reappeared.

Damn.

"Move."

I moved, but not because he told me to. I dragged down the rest of the path because if I didn't keep moving, I'd pass out and melt into the scorching ground. We made it to the moat of leaping flames encircling his castle. I remembered giving a weak thumbs up, then the world went sideways. I tumbled toward the tongues of fizzing fire. Talons clutched and everything went away.

***

I woke in a strange place. Strange because I'd never been there before, but also weird because, well, it was pretty. The massive bed beneath me threatened to swallow me with its fluffy layers. The air settled like a cool hand on my skin. A fountain of actual water bubbled and flowed in a circle on the floor. The narrow channel gurgled and trickled around the generous bed. Ornate little bridges crossed the current at each of the cardinal directions. Soft, colorful still life paintings hung on the walls depicting dark-skinned fruits and thickly-petaled flowers from the destroyed Night Gardens. A tall, gilded cage resting on a delicately carved pedestal held a rare greenish-blue volcanus gecko. The tiny fire-breather opened one tired eye, gave me a glittering glance, then sealed his lid shut again. Intricately woven rugs covered the stone floor giving the roughly-hewn room a softer feel. Heavy, red curtains partially hid the sharp, twisted landscape of smoke and fire on the other side of a wide balcony.

"What the Wells?" I sat up and took a deep breath of slightly moistened air. I coughed, clutching my dry throat. What I would have done for a juicy watermelon pixie right then. My gaze drifted to the circle of water as I seriously considered drinking the floor.

A massive door swung open and my least favorite person stepped through. At least he was holding a goblet of liquid.

"From our deepest well," he growled. Hamus stepped over the rippling blue circle of water and handed me the cup. The King of Demons had made it clear on many occasions that the only good Lilith was a dead Lilith. A little poison in a beautiful goblet was a quick, easy way to end me. Unfortunately, thirst ruled the moment. I drained the vessel.

"Is this—" I looked around the room.

"My private space." Anger incinerated his words as he spoke them.

If I could have levitated off the bed I would have, but given my strength at that moment, I settled for a clumsy shuffle across the bedspread and a less than graceful swing over the side. My feet touched the floor and I stood only to tip sideways again. Hamus's hand shot out and caught me. He glowered at me with the glowing embers of his eyes, but there was no actual fire to them. There was no fire to any of him. The ever-present flames that danced between his horns like a burning crown had extinguished. His hands did not blaze. Even his massive hooves had lost their sparks.

His hand, where it touched me, still burned with a natural heat. Standing this close to him was like standing next to a thermal vent. A tall, wide-shouldered vent with an anvil of a jaw and a square bottom lip meant for scolding, reprimanding, doling out orders. Not for kissing. Never for kissing. But every time I looked at it, I couldn't look away.

"Lilith," he snarled. "Did you not hear what I said?" His mouth steamed with reproach. I almost wanted to continue my bad behavior to see what he'd do with those super-heated lips. What would he do with those molten hands? I could throw the delicate drinking glass across the room and find out.

"I know it is hard for a succubus to stay focused, but try and marshal your thoughts." The fire demon sizzled with restraint, but he leaned over me like a landslide. He rolled his shoulders and cracked his thick neck.

"What?" My lagging brain stumbled back over the words he'd just said. "*You* marshal *your* thoughts. I'm not the one that mismanaged this scenario." I took leave of my senses and jabbed a finger in his radiating chest. "The Council knew something was wrong with the Underhill months ago, maybe longer. When you sent me to Florida, you knew."

Small blue flames flickered to life in his eyes, but his thoughts seemed to have bent inward. I watched as his gaze focused on something in the past.

"Yes." He spat the word out like a bony bit of pixie wing. I wanted to enjoy the concession. I'd never heard Hamus concede to anything, but he'd offered it too willingly. The elder standing before me hunched under a heavy weight. He glanced at me in all his destructive thantos glory—then hung his head. Was that...shame? His frame drooped until his scaled face came within touching range. The plated bridge of his nose hovered inches from mine. If I wanted to, I could have licked the spikes at the edge of his jaw. Would he like that? Would it turn his thoughts to me and away from all this devastation?

I actively pushed the thought from my distracted brain.

"What has happened?" I asked gently, but fastened my gaze on him like a hawk. A lie-detecting hawk with years of experience with disinformation.

When Hamus looked up again, he was a different person. A stranger. Someone with feelings.

"We thought we had control," he whispered as if the walls were listening.

"Control of what?"

"The Underhill." His eyes widened like something horrible dangled before them.

"The Underhill did this to itself?" I raised my hand to his scorching cheek. I almost touched him, but years of blistering anger, blazing hot bullying stopped me.

"Yes." His horns dipped low as he nodded once. "We tried to stop it and, when we realized we couldn't, we tried to evacuate everyone, but...the Underhill closed the portals." I didn't know what to be more shocked by—what he went on to describe, or how Hamus, King of the Fire Drakes, Lord of Flames, Council

Elder, had fallen so far that he would confide in me—a lowly Lilith. Someone he clearly loathed.

I hugged myself as he explained how the events had unfolded, the earthquakes, the disintegrating infrastructure, whole levels collapsing. All while I'd been sitting on a beach in Florida sipping Mai Tais and reminiscing with my old college roommate.

"We couldn't escape to the other Faerie Lands, but we couldn't stay inside its rapidly condensing body. The bones of the ceilings grew tendons. The walls grew flesh. Every refuge was swallowed by muscles and arteries. The thumping of its heart became unbearable." He looked at me as though I were a friend to whom he could bare his soul. But Hamus Flamesire had not earned my friendship. We could have been friends...could have been more than friends, but he'd never allowed it. Now, when our world lay in ruins—now, when his sphere of power had crumbled—he looked me in the eye. Saw me. Spoke to me without rebuke. Showed me kindness. "We tore our way out, taking as many as we could with us." Trauma fed the flames in his eyes. Hamus was the epitome of strength. Seeing him like this was almost more horrifying than witnessing the ruins of our home. But, for some reason, I breathed every breath of this moment as if it were a gift. As awful as everything was, I didn't want this tiny piece of reality between us to end. This...bond.

His head jerked up. His fierce eyes focused on me. *Oh, Lesser Gods.* Was he snapping out of it? Was he coming to his senses. I pictured myself skinned and tossed into the burning moat below for having witnessed his moment of weakness. Or stamped into a bloody pulp and kicked into the fountain circling his bed.

Why would a fire demon have a fountain in his bedroom?

I could see the here-and-now in his eyes. He was back from his dark reminiscence.

Welp, if I was about to have my ass handed to me, I was going to ask the questions I'd always wanted to ask. Rapid fire.

"Why do you hate Liliths?"

The demon's molten brows had cooled to the gray of incinerated bodies. They crunched as they crowded low over his eyes. Hamus regarded me from beneath that familiar frown. And then, he did something utterly unexpected. He thought about it.

I blinked in the silence.

I shifted my weight from foot to foot.

How long did it take to contemplate one small question?

"I do not hate Liliths."

It was my turn to frown. I didn't hide my skeptical look. This fiery pile of disdain had shown me nothing but cruelty my entire life. Who hates a kid? This guy. Literally. I'd been an orphan with no support, no home, no one to give a bat's ass if I lived or died. And he'd gone out of his way to ostracize me, to devalue me, to sweep me aside whenever the opportunity arose. It had only gotten worse as I grew into adulthood. Had I not had Peg Powler looking in on me from time to time, I would have rotted from the inside out. I would have become the thing the human scrolls described. Heartless. A predator with no other calling in life, but to do harm. I thought of the Lilith I'd visited on the lonely mountaintop in West Virginia. That could have been me.

When I'd left for college, I'd thought the demon would bar the doors and lock me out. But Peg had made plans for me in the program. She'd arranged my education in the human world. She'd set me up in the fae laboratories. My skill set had proven to be more useful in the field, but regardless of that, I'd succeeded despite Hamus Flamesire.

"So…it's just me…that you hate."

I watched him watching me. Studying me. I refused to look away. I'd never stared at him this long. As a result, I began to see the finer details of his face. He had long lashes, the color of soot, hidden beneath his muscular frown. The hollows of his cheek bones held more than vicious shadows. He had a dusting of dark beard there as well, shaved to accentuate the drastic planes of his face. As my gaze wandered, I noticed that the angry, segmented arrow of his nose, the jutting cliff of his chin, every inch of his brutal face was held together by diamonds. Or rather a diamond pattern of scales, small and even and reflecting the low light like stitched satin. I'd always thought that sheen was just sweat. It wasn't. Up close, Hamus was kind of beautiful. Deadly, but handsome in a savage way.

"I don't hate you either…Lilith."

I sucked in a breath.

The way he'd said my name. My common, featureless name. The same name every member of my genetic family went by.

He'd made it sound personal. Private. Like something he kept in a box, hidden away even from himself.

I gaped at the ruthless elder, the callous man. Something in his tone reminded me of that strange, desperate call I'd felt in Florida the night I'd almost lost my life.

My eyes burned, then swam. Tears flooded my vision. Confusion clouded my brain. And my heart—my heart did the dumbest thing of all.

It opened.

14

SALAMANDER

100% North African Fire Salamander

Fire. An element I'd taken for granted. A source of warmth. A means of light. A useful thing, but a substance to be avoided in large quantity. Fire was, by nature, dangerous. And yet, as I stood gazing into the cauldrons of Hamus's eyes, I wanted to burn.

He didn't hate me. Why did that small bit of news fill me with relief? He hadn't said that he liked me. This wasn't exactly a declaration of love from a man I already felt deep affection for. This was hateful Hamus, the fractious fire drake who'd made my life miserable on many occasions. Sure, he was hot. He'd fathered many lines of fae. Women from all the great fae families had willingly spread their legs for him. Yes, I'd sworn never to be one of those women, but I wasn't blind. I'd appreciated his...physical attributes on more than one occasion.

A maelstrom of confusion stirred to life inside me.

He didn't hate me.

But he didn't like me. He didn't love me. Daniel loved me. Why did it feel so good not to be hated by this demon in particular?

A strange supplicating impulse flickered to life inside me. It crept through my mind on scraped knees. A beggar of an emotion pleading to be fed. It ached for attention, it itched to be indulged, it craved correction, it pined for punishment and pleaded for praise. I'd experienced it with the Immortal Serpent, but now I knew what I'd felt with the naga had only scratched the surface of a depthless desire. The feeling spread through me like an endocrine wildfire. Was it new? Or had the roots of it been buried inside me for years?

I looked deeply into the flames of the demon's eyes. I saw the agonized elder, the besieged ruler. I saw the man hiding his true feelings for me. And then, I saw the deep, imprisoned thing.

Daddy. It whispered through me. Not paternal in the real sense, but protective, stern, controlling. It hovered behind iron bars waiting for the right hand to unlock its cage. Hamus sucked in a breath as I unfolded the secret at the center of all secrets. It was the reason I'd wanted his acceptance so badly but would never admit it. It was the reason why I'd delighted in the news that he didn't hate me. If he didn't hate me, then maybe he approved of me. If he approved of me, then maybe...possibly...he thought I was a good girl.

Desire tore through me. Eros rolled like a tidal wave from my neglected core.

"Lilith, no."

In that moment, "no" was not an option. There were too many things I wanted and now I knew why I wanted them from him.

"Lilith, there are things—" He struggled against the waves of desire that would have put a lesser fey on his ass. "—we must speak of." The breathless tone in his voice added fuel to my blazing flesh. I wanted to affect him. I thought back to all the times his fire had flared when I'd come near. Yes, they were angry flames, but I'd affected him.

Yet, none of his past reactions compared to now. The exquisite, dangerous, burning now.

He fought the irrepressible lust wrapping around us.

Silly demon.

I slipped past his tensing arms. Pressed my chilled skin to his. "Lilith."

I slid my hands along the scorched hills and valleys of the body I'd wanted for so long. The muscles I'd yearned to lick. I leaned into the cock I'd wanted to suck so hard it made my mouth water.

"Yes...Daddy."

I said it.

The butterflies in my stomach pumped their wings so quickly I thought I would lift off the floor.

He gripped me. Anchored me. His fingers dug into my cool flesh.

"Say it again," he rumbled in my ear. I became a fountain of desire. A geyser of rhapsody. My eros rolled over us, devouring the demon. Devouring me.

"Whatever you want, Daddy," I whispered and wrapped my thin arms around his giant neck. Those words seemed to be the trigger he'd been waiting for someone to pull.

His mouth engulfed mine. His burning hot tongue plunged past my lips. For a brief second, I thought I might suffocate as he feasted so deeply. My throat clenched...and then I surrendered to the kiss.

"Good girl." He pulled away long enough to reward me for my small submission and then plundered me again. In all my encounters with lovers, I'd always been the consumer, never the consumed. I hung from his arms as he took what he wanted. I opened my vast stores of mana. He shuddered through the wave of power, then his sizzling hand roamed, searching my curves as if they were a treasure he'd lost in the dark.

"Lilith."

Why was he saying my name so much? Each time, it travelled from my ears straight to my heart and then lower. I needed to be seen. I wanted affection. I craved his control. I yearned to be admired. I needed authority. I wanted a firm hand. A loving, firm hand to roam my body just like that. To keep me in check. To reward me for being a good girl. And punish me when I was bad.

"We cannot do this." His bruising lips left mine. His hands released me so quickly I almost collapsed to the floor.

"Why not?" I stole the space he'd just created between us. I pressed against him again. Grazed him with the diamond-hard tips of my breasts. I wanted to show him what a good girl I could be.

"Because—" The fiery crown between his horns ignited, bathing me in heat. He eased me away from him. "I promised to protect you."

The carnival ride of desire spinning inside me screeched to a halt.

"What?" What had he just said? "You promised?" I stumbled back. "To protect me?" My body ached with unrequited eros. "Who did you promise?" The question felt like a ghost being released from the fleshy plane. One I hadn't even known was there.

His eyes slid to the secret he'd kept locked in that spiky, bone box of a skull. I thought to slap the answer out of it. To grab his horns and shake until the truth felt out.

He caught me in a gaze with such force, it almost knocked me from my feet.

"Your mother."

"My—" The breath left my body. It followed the ghost out the window into a world that no longer made sense. Why would my mother even talk to Hamus much less bind him in a promise. What gave this monstrous man, this—this vile demon the right to speak of my mother.

"She was a Lilith." I summoned enough wind to speak. "Why would you care about her unborn daughter?"

His gaze softened. Deep gray lashes swept low over the banking bonfires of his eyes.

"Because I loved her." The confession fell from him like a great weight.

I backed away. My feet hit the bed. I fell into the cloud of softness, but it wasn't a welcome softness. It was a trap, a tangle of blankets, a quagmire of pillows. I scrambled over the sinking, feathered landscape. Over the bed that wasn't designed for him. That bed would burn if he tried to lie in it.

"Who was this bed made for?" I demanded as I dragged myself over the side and onto the floor. "Why do you have a fountain in the Domain of Fire?" My foot splashed in the bubbling water as I tumbled over one of the narrow bridges. "Why does the King of Flames have a rushing channel of spring water in his very sanctuary?" I shouted. Why couldn't I get my feet under me? Why was I here in this place with the most odious demon in all of Faerie?

He took a step as if to offer me a hand up. I shuffled away from him, which put my back to a wall. He stopped. His hooves scraped the stone floor as he backed away just a little.

"I have the fountain—" his eyes drifted to the circle "—because she loved water."

My heart hurt in places I didn't know existed.

"The bed was for her." His throat seemed to constrict around his words. "It was for Lilith."

There it was. My name. Spoken from his lips. Like a prayer to the Father Who Turned Away. But he wasn't speaking of me. It was her. My mother. The woman I'd never known, but he had. It seemed so horribly unfair. The demon had made his way into the one location where I had no defenses. The womb of wombs. The place where I kept my mother.

A horrible thought spread its sludge through me. My skin crawled. My stomach knotted. I had no choice...I had to ask.

"Are you the reason my mother is dead?" I gasped, clutching my hands to my heart. "Are you my father?"

He reeled back from me just as something large enough to have its own gravity crashed to the ground somewhere past the small canyon in which the castle stood. The impact shattered the steaming earth.

Hamus raced to the cage holding the Volcanus Gecko and ripped its door open. The brightly-colored lizard bolted from its prison. To my surprise, another smaller creature, maybe a sala-mander, darted from the gilded cell as well. It must have been buried beneath the larger lizard. Another secret. The delicate thing wound down the pedestal in a flash of black and yellow splotches and disappeared under the door.

A heartbeat later, shards of hardened lava pelted the stone walls of the fortress. Burning hot chunks of molten rock hurled through the open balcony.

Hamus dove for me, wrapping my body in his arms, turning his back to the destruction, shielding me against his chest.

The citadel shook with a second tremendous blast. Stone shattered.

Another collision—this one bigger. Cliffs fell. A pale, many-throated wail rose in the distance as flightless fae refugees fell from the crumbling caves.

"What is that?" I squirmed in the prison of his arms. Shock and horror ripped through me like twin talons.

The stronghold, the pinnacle of the Kingdom of Flames, the seat of Hamus's power, the last refuge of the Maryland Fae...cracked.

"The sky is falling," he answered.

THE END

I know I talk a tough game about hating humans, but you know I don't really hate you. I just envy you. At the moment, I really envy the fact that you can live in a non-sentient environment. One that won't collapse on you from a broken heart at any second.

The other fae, however, do hate you. Don't get me wrong, they'll take your tourist money, but don't expect much more.

Imagine their chagrin when they realize that their home, their very existence may depend on one sneaky human with stolen magic and a marriage proposal. So, stop squirming and listen up. This is about to get interesting.

Excerpt

Wedding the Warlock – The FAEverse Chronicles Book 3

Black veins travelled the roads of his face. Magic skittered under his skin like rats in the walls. Stolen magic. Forces he couldn't possibly control had the human in a head lock of distorted time and ruptured space. The poison crept like a warning to the corners of his eyes. Down his neck to the fossil permanently secured to his sternum. The only thing more treacherous than a human is a human with power.

The male named Daniel stepped from the shadows. An uninvited guest with pools of peril glimmering in his eyes.

"You have no place here," I assured him. "Leave now and you may keep your wretched life." This infidel deserved a painful death for even thinking of setting foot in my domain. But killing him would upset Lilith. I could not bear the thought of her in any more pain. But this brazen human must be removed. He could not be allowed to reach her. I had failed her mother. I would not fail Lilith. The Father Who Turned Away had blessed me with another chance, a second bonding. A thing so rare as to not even be dreamt of by fae-kind. Lilith has given me nothing but hope, renewal, love. And I have met her with anger, violence, rejection.

She is my charge. My mate. Mine.

I will never give her up. Certainly, not to this sickly sorcerer. This malignant man, befouled by the power he'd taken without right. Corrupted to his withering core by the ill-fitting mantle of ancient magic. That form of enchantment had been scrubbed from the Ways long ago for good reason.

The human shook his head slowly. Refusal. Tenacity twisted his bloodless mouth into a brash smile. Daniel the Defiled was resolute in his purpose. That resolve would be his ruin.

I could wait. Let it rot him from the inside out. Or I could burn him to ash where he stood and suffer the consequences with my mate.

A flash of movement caught my eye above us. A glint of winding scales lost to the dark and ravaged sky. It offered a third option.

With a thought, a simple projection of will, the Whisk Drake streaked through the calamity of clouds tumbling overhead. A missile of blackest night, my best and strongest dragon. She tucked her wings in flat to build speed.

"This is your last warning," I growled.

Daniel climbed the rise in front of me, claiming the high ground, no doubt securing a vantage point to better survey my land.

This would be gratifying. My drake would rip him limb from limb. An accident. A hungry drake. A meaty human morsel still days from complete spoilage.

The swift beast raced toward the ground.

Wait, I whispered.

The clever creature held her course.

Wait. I timed her dive to perfection.

She trusted me. She had relied on my guardianship and direction since her hatching. I'd trained her. Honed her. My beautiful weapon. My lethal proxy.

Now!

Onyx wings unfurled, trapping the rising heat. Curving. Slicing through steam. Sliding on air. Talons out. Teeth gleaming.

Her trajectory was flawless. In an exquisite maneuver of muscles and wings, she reached for the human who stood vulnerable on the bluff of broken ground—a fitting end for the interloper who'd laid an illegitimate claim on my mate's heart.

And then the universe shattered.

Lightning screamed. Air bled. The fabric of reality peeled away as the forces of unmaking devoured the space just above the human. There was no warning. My drake slid into the wreckage of molecules. Her sleek body unraveled as if torn asunder by a thousand iron blades. Her quivering body spilled to the ground in a rainstorm of wasted flesh. Hot blood bathed my face, my neck, my chest.

"Night Mother," I swore as the mana of my beloved drake passed through me into the Realms Phantasmal. I gaped. Gore dripped into my mouth salty and rich with the tang of liver and the bitterness of kidneys. I breathed her essence. Let it ignite my deepest furnace. Lava woke inside me. Fire trembled along my skin. I drank the rush of fire. Gulped it until it utterly consumed me.

"You will burn."

I reveled in the promise for freshly crisped flesh. My mouth watered. My cock hardened.

Hamus?

My mate's new, inner voice echoed weakly in my head. It lacked force. She had not yet learned to project her full presence. I swept her aside as death-lust washed over me.

"Turn to sweet ash for me." I opened wide my blazing soul and drowned the man in flames. I poured myself out like an erupting star. I scorched the ground on which he stood. Burned the air. Ignited the shadows from which he'd appeared. I let my rage run like a river of magma down to the last smoldering embers.

I breathed the delicious char, licked the cinders from the air, and waited for my reward—his blackened bones.

The flames leapt and danced and died away.

Daniel the Defiled stood in the ashes of his clothes, unscathed and unrelenting. This could not be.

"You will never have her." My declaration rang from cliff to canyon, but something akin to fear planted its seeds in my gut.

The black snakes of diseased power wormed beneath Daniel's skin.

"She's already mine."

The human smiled.

Also By

Hunter J. Skye

The Hell Gate Series:

A Glimmer of Ghosts – book 1

A Shiver of Shadows – book 2

Gauntlet of Light – book 2.5

A Rapture of Wraiths – book 3 *(coming in 2025)*

The FAEverse Chronicles:

Seducing the Serpent

Devouring the Demon

Wedding the Warlock *(coming in 2025)*

About the Author

Coastal Virginia native and America's Next Great Author reality tv show semi-finalist, Hunter J. Skye, was born with a rare nightmare disorder and raised in a haunted Victorian home. Those two factors predestined her to write dark and twisted paranormal tales.

With a Bachelor of the Fine Arts, Hunter first went into museology, but her love of the written word drew her back to the keyboard. She now writes full-time and ghost-hunts on the weekends.

Hunter enjoys nature, stargazing, all things paranormal, and is a proud Jeep Girl. For more about Hunter's books or her dubious sense of humor, go to: www.hunterskye.com.